TROUBLE

Also by Bali Rai:

Soccer Squad: Starting Eleven
Soccer Squad: Missing!
Soccer Squad: Stars!
Soccer Squad: Glory!

For older readers

(Un)arranged Marriage
The Crew
Rani and Sukh
The Whisper
The Last Taboo
The Angel Collector
City of Ghosts
Killing Honour
Fire City

TROUBLE

Two tales from Devana High

BALI RAI

Tamarind

TROUBLE
A TAMARIND BOOK 978 1 848 53120 8

Published in Great Britain by Tamarind Books,
an imprint of Random House Children's Publishers UK
A Random House Group Company

Grace first published in Great Britain in 2004 as *Concrete Chips* by Hodder Children's Books
Dean first published in Great Britain in 2005 as *Sold as Seen* by Hodder Children's Books

Tamarind edition published 2013

1 3 5 7 9 10 8 6 4 2

Set in Garamond Reg

Tamarind Books are published by Random House Children's Publishers UK,
61–63 Uxbridge Road, London W5 5SA

www.tamarindbooks.co.uk
www.randomhousechildrens.co.uk
www.randomhouse.co.uk

Addresses for companies within The Random House Group Limited can be found at:
www.randomhouse.co.uk/offices.htm

THE RANDOM HOUSE GROUP Limited Reg. No. 954009

A CIP catalogue record for this book is available from the British Library.

Printed and bound by CPI Group (UK) Ltd, Croydon, CR0 4YY

CONTENTS

CONTENTS

GRACE

To everyone who attended Judgemeadow, 1983–1988.
Even the teachers . . .

ONE

'Come on, Grace! You're going to be late . . .'

I groaned and turned my head, pulling the pillow over it. My bed was so warm.

'Grace . . .'

I looked out from under my pillow.

'Urrggh . . .' I groaned.

'Grace!'

Just ten more minutes. Just ten, I thought. The world wasn't going anywhere, was it? Stinky school could wait . . .

'Get up, you lazy little . . .'

This time Dad's voice was right outside my bedroom door. I blinked at the light coming in through the blinds and groaned again before slipping a leg out of bed to test the world and see if it was ready for me.

'OK. OK. I'm coming,' I grunted at my dad, flopping out of bed.

* * *

Twenty minutes later I had showered and dressed and was walking down to the bus stop, stuffing a piece of toast into my mouth. My skirt was twisted round the wrong way and my jumper felt like it was trying to strangle me. I reached the bus stop and threw my bag down, sighing. Another stinky Monday morning.

Dean and Jit walked up as I was wiping bread-crumbs from my mouth. They always walked to my bus stop each morning. God knows why – I haven't even got the energy to get out of bed most mornings and those two walk for fifteen minutes just to catch the wrong bus. Boys . . .

'Late as usual,' said Jit and grinned.

'Fashionably,' I told him, noticing that his hair looked like it had been cut by a blind man with the shakes.

'Did little *Jitty-kins* lose his comb?' I asked in my worst 'stupid-girly' voice. 'Or is that your attempt at boy-band fashion?'

Dean laughed at Jit.

'Man, school ain't even started yet and you're getting dissed already . . .'

'*Wha*'? And I suppose that jumper is a fashion statement?' Jit replied, grinning at me.

I looked at my jumper, pretending that it looked fine.

'What's wrong with it, stupid boy . . . ?'

'You might wanna take it off and try again, Grace . . .' said Dean.

'Oh get stuffed, you little—' I began, only to be cut off by a couple of squealing boys wearing full uniform.

'*She's got her jumper on inside out . . .*'

I looked at my clothes again. They were right. In my rush to catch the bus I had forgotten to turn my jumper the right way round. I grinned at Jit and Dean to hide my embarrassment.

'S'meant to be inside out,' I told them, foolishly.

'Yeah, *right*,' laughed Jit.

I gave him a stare. I didn't care how good looking he was, he wasn't getting away with laughing at my appearance.

'It's a new design,' I said.

'Don't even come with that nonsense, Grace,' said Dean, unimpressed. 'Just take it off and turn it the right way round . . .'

My name is Grace because I was born on a Monday and my grandmother was called Nina, which is

Russian for Grace – or so my mum tells me. I'm twelve years old but don't let that fool you. I'm like a mini-adult according to my dad, the product of a generation 'ruined by the internet and mobile telephones . . .' My mum and dad are both thirty-eight and they always bang on about how in 'their day' the youth were more rebellious, always protesting and going to festivals, dancing in the mud.

My dad works as an architect with his best friend, Tommy. He works from home and is always 'just about to start work', normally with a cup of coffee in his hands. My mum is a social worker and spends a lot more time out of the house than my dad. She comes home stressed-out most evenings and she's the bad cop to my dad's good cop. If I ever want something that I'm not supposed to have, like a new top or something, I ask my dad because he's always busy and says yes to almost anything, only to get told off by my mum when she gets home. I get my dad into a lot of trouble but he doesn't mind. I think he enjoys it.

Our house is in a nice area, according to most of my friends, and they usually spend quite a lot of time in our cellar which is huge. There's a pool table in there, and sofas and a telly, so we use it as a hangout, which is lovely, apart from when my dad walks in and starts trying to act like he's 'in with the kids' by talking in rhyme like a rapper or '*cuffing*' the boys and telling them to '*cool out, man*'. That's when I wish I had a normal dad, instead of the weirdo that I do have, with his Jesus sandals and Bob Dylan T-shirts and shiny cords. I do love him to bits though, *groovy* bead necklaces and all.

I've got five really good friends from school. There's Dean who's thirteen and thinks he's an MC – he's even got a stupid name, MC D-C. His mum works with mine and his dad is cool. He owns a bar in town and he has the nicest smile.

Imtiaz is thirteen too. He's really tall and good look- ing, and one of those boys who's good at everything, from football to art. All the girls like him – he's like the most popular boy in school. I don't fancy him though – he's not my type. He's uptight and always trying to act older than he is. His favourite phrase is 'grow up, we're not kids any more' which he mostly uses when he's talking to me or Dean. Or Jit.

Jit is the same age as Dean and Imtiaz. His mum is single – she works in a supermarket, and there's loads of stuff going on between Jit, his mum and the rest of his family, I think. I'm not too sure because Jit never really talks about his home life. He clams up when anyone talks about families and stuff. He's always getting into trouble with the teachers and the older lads at school. Usually he gets Dean into trouble too. Jit's really clever but he hides it and he picks on me all the time. In a nice way though. We have a love/hate thing, according to my dad, who gets on really well with him. Hannah thinks Jit fancies me 'cos he's always round our house, even when the others aren't there.

The girls are called Suky and Hannah and they're both thirteen too. Suky is really tall and skinny and athletic. She's like the girl version of Imtiaz. She's the leader whenever we argue and she's always beating the boys in races and other sporty stuff. She even beat Imtiaz in 'keep-ups' with a football, which really wound him up for a while. Not too long though. He and Suky are really close and I think they would make a good couple. Suky wants to be an actress when she's older.

Hannah's a good laugh. She's really clever and sometimes she's a bit fiery but mostly she's really cool. Her mum works in the same supermarket as Jit's mum. Jit and Hannah grew up together, going to the same school since they were five, along with Dean. Suky, Imtiaz and me went to the same schools too, so when we got to Year Seven we were like two little gangs joining up into one. Hannah wants to be a journalist and is desperate to set up a school newspaper, only our principal, Mr Black, claims there isn't enough time or money to do one.

That's our gang then. I suppose I should get back to the story, really . . .

TWO

The bus took twenty-five minutes to get through the traffic before it reached the school and by that time it was full of kids shouting and screaming and throwing things out of the window. Like a zoo but on wheels, with an upper and lower deck. I got up slowly and followed the boys, catching my foot against a giant black sports bag that had been left, thoughtfully, in the aisle. I swore and heard a deep, 'I'm nearly a man' laugh. It was the bag's owner, an older boy, Jason Patel.

'Wanna watch where you're goin', sexy . . .' he said to me with a smirk.

'Get stuffed . . .'

'*Easy* – gal thinks she's funny, innit . . .' he said to his mates, who all joined him in laughing at me.

'I'm sorry?' I asked, pretending that I didn't understand what he meant.

'*I'm sorry* . . .' he mimicked.

'Come on, Grace,' said Jit, from the stairwell.

'Better go join yer boyfriend, sexy . . .' smiled Jason.

'And *you'd* better get to the dentist. Yellow teeth . . . Big no-no.'

I walked away quickly as Jason's face turned red and his mates started laughing and telling him to clean his teeth. He called me a rude name as I went downstairs and got off the bus. Jit and Dean were standing in the bus shelter waiting for me.

'Let's try and get to school on time for once,' said Jit.

The stop was about a quarter of a mile from the school gates and we walked slowly down the road, other kids running past us to get in before the registration bell went. Jason and his mates ran past too, calling me names. Jit called Jason a few back. But then Jason stopped and turned round.

'You what?' he shouted.

'You're in the dog-do now!' Dean grinned.

Jit looked like he was about to apologize but instead he shrugged and carried on walking. Jason shouted something about 'another time' and ran off after his friends, his bag bouncing on his back.

'Fool!' spat Jit.

'Don't worry about it,' replied Dean. 'If he's so bad, he would have dealt with it right here . . .'

'I ain't scared of him . . .' said Jit.

'God – you two are *soooo* tough,' I laughed, trying to wind them up.

'Shut up and wipe the crumbs off your face,' said Jit, smiling.

'*Stinky git* . . .'

I didn't have time to finish because the bell sounded and we were only just at the gates. Mr Black was standing at the main entrance, looking at his watch and shaking his head. As we walked up he tut-tutted.

'And good evening to you three,' he said, straightening his tie knot.

'Bus was late . . .' mumbled Jit, not looking at him.

'I believe that if you had caught an earlier bus—' began Black, but Dean cut him off. Big mistake.

'There was traffic, sir!'

'Now, now, Dean. We don't interrupt people when they are speaking, do we?'

'Nossir.'

'Because that would be very rude of us, now wouldn't it . . .?'

'Yessir.'

'Right then. Now get to your form rooms and if I see you dawdle into school tomorrow, I'll have to give you detention . . .'

'*But sir*—' I began, only to be interrupted by the man who had told Dean that it was wrong.

'Firm but fair, young lady. Firm but fair . . .'

'Unlike your belly,' whispered Jit as Mr Black walked out of earshot.

'Unlike *which* one – the firm or the fair?' I asked him.

'Definitely the *firm*. Black needs some serious exercise . . .'

'You'll be like that one day,' I said with a grin.

'Maybe so,' replied Jit, 'but I won't be walking round with toast stuck to me face like you, will I?'

'*Dissed* . . .' laughed Dean, giving me a bear hug.

'Gerroff . . .!'

Mrs Dooher, our form tutor, was reading out names as we joined our classmates. As usual, I went and sat down with Suky and Hannah, at a table just in front of the boys. Imtiaz shook his head and laughed as we walked in.

'One of these days you lot will be on time,' he said, like he was our dad or something.

'Just 'cos you like to get here before the caretaker don't mean we have to,' replied Jit, winking at me.

I couldn't wink back because I can't wink. Whenever I try, I look like a constipated baboon with heartburn. Mrs Dooher looked up from her register and smiled. She was my favourite teacher, a bit like a surrogate mother, with her soft Liverpool accent and stories of being asked out by some old bloke called Paul McCartney who used to be in a band called The Beatles. I had to raid my dad's music collection to find out who he was. A pop star but a real one with talent – not like the rubbish nowadays, according to my dad. Mrs Dooher gave us the dreaded announcement – late lunch week. Again. Then she stood up and shuffled over to where we were sitting.

'I'm going to have to tell you off for being late again', she said with a smile.

'We're sorry,' I told her, answering for Jit and Dean too.

'You're always sorry, Grace. I can't keep making excuses for you all . . .'

'Won't happen again, miss,' Dean replied. 'Honest.'

'I dunno,' she said, smiling again.

Dean grinned and then got up and gave her a hug.

'You're *lurrvely . . .*' he told her, in a silly accent.

'You cheeky *get . . .*' she replied.

'Do we have to be on late lunches again, miss?' he asked her.

The others didn't hear him. They were busy gossiping about school stuff. But I wanted to know what he was talking about.

'It's on the rota, Dean. That's the way it goes . . .'

'But *miss* – the food's always cold and that . . .'

'And *what . . .*?'

'I'm sorry?'

Mrs Dooher smiled again. 'You say "*and that*" after every sentence. I was just wondering "*and what*" exactly,' she asked.

'It's just street banter, you get me?' replied Dean.

'Do I?' grinned Mrs Dooher.

'What?' asked Dean, confused.

'*Get you.* Do I *really* get you . . .?'

'Oh you're just takin' the p—'

'*Dean!*' replied Mrs Dooher, pretending to be stern.

'The mickey, I mean.'

'That's better,' she said. 'Now get off to your lessons and leave me to prepare for the nightmare that is Year Ten.'

The others were already on their way to lessons as I pulled Dean to one side and asked him why he was bothered by being on late lunch all of a sudden.

'The food's nasty,' he told me. 'All cold and that . . .'

'And *what*?' I replied, a feeble attempt to continue a bad joke, I know.

'Grace . . .'

'But we've had a lunch rota since we got here,' I said.

'Yeah – I know that but it don't mean we have to like it. You remember that silly rhyme – *School Dinners*?'

'Yeah. "*Concrete chips, concrete chips. Sloppy semolina . . .*"'

'Relax, Grace. Ain't no need to make it rain by singing the thing . . .'

I stopped singing and pouted at him but he just ignored me. Silly boy!

'Well I reckon we should complain . . .' he said.

'Who to, Dean? No one is going to change the rules because of us.'

'Don't mean we shouldn't complain,' he moaned,

as we walked after the rest of our form group.

I sang the silly rhyme all the way to French, in a French accent, until Dean put me in a headlock to make me stop.

THREE

We were standing in the dinner queue later on when Dean started going on about cold food again.

'See what I mean? Everyone else has had their food but we've got to wait till last and then all we get to eat is cold chips.'

'Speak for yourself,' I told him. 'I don't eat chips.'

'Well what are you gonna eat today then?'

I waited a few moments until we'd reached the service hatch and looked at what was on offer. Dean's concrete chips were there, together with something that looked like it might be lasagne. There were two fish cakes in a separate steel tray, some burnt sausages and what seemed to be pizza portions too. I couldn't tell because the topping was black and crispy. Beside these tempting dishes sat a tray of Cellophane-wrapped sandwiches with handwritten stickers telling us what they had in them. Egg mayonnaise, tuna salad, cheese salad, ham salad. Even *salad* salad for the vegans. The bread looked like it had been stepped on by an elephant and the plastic was all sweaty. I turned my nose up and picked up a bruised banana, two apples and a bottle of water.

'I'm on a diet,' I told Dean.

'See? The food is *rank*,' he replied, looking at his wedge of looky-likey lasagne and brittle potato.

'Oh shut up and quit complaining, you girl!'

'Well, would *you* eat this?'

I turned up my nose again. 'No – I told you I'm on a diet!'

We walked over to the table where the rest of our friends were sitting. Imtiaz and Suky were whispering something to each other and Hannah was telling Jit about how much the school needed its own paper. Jit looked bored as he tried to spear his chips with a fork. One of the chips flew off the plate and landed on the table, making Jit and Hannah laugh.

'Are you two ever gonna grow up?' asked Imtiaz, looking disgusted.

'*Are you two ever gonna grow up!*' mimicked Jit, grinning.

'See what I mean?' continued Imtiaz, looking at Suky.

As Dean and I sat down, Jit picked up the offending chip and threw it at Imtiaz's head. It bounced off his temple and landed in the plate of a lad called Mohammed.

'Oi!'

'Easy, Mohammed,' laughed Jit. 'No need to get your panties in a—'

'KOONER!!!!!'

Jit groaned. The shout had come from Mr Herbert, pupil enemy No. 1 and all round grump.

'Food is for eating,' Mr Herbert bellowed across three tables, spitting everywhere.

'Yessir,' mumbled Jit.

'Don't you "yessir" me, young man! World full of starving people and here you are throwing precious food around!'

'Ain't like I can post it to 'em, is it?' said Jit, making everyone under the age of sixteen snigger.

'Looks like it was posted to *us*,' added Dean, just loud enough to be heard.

Herbert's face began to redden, 'MY OFFICE!'

I looked at Jit and shook my head. Jit shrugged his shoulders and stood up.

'Can't even finish me dinner . . .' he said. 'What is this – *prison*?'

'You too, Dean Chambers,' continued Herbert.

'Ah, sir!' moaned Dean, throwing his fork down on his plate.

'Don't "Ah sir" me. As if I haven't a million and one things to do with my lunch time already.'

Dean swore under his breath, stood up and slammed his chair under the table, sending my water spilling. I moved my legs out of its path as it poured off the table but I didn't say anything to Dean. He was angry enough.

Then I did something really stupid.

'You know, Mr Herbert, lunch is a basic human right,' I said, sounding really smarmy.

Mr Herbert looked at me in shock. I think he expected lip from Jit and Dean but from a nice girl like me? I sat and waited for him to say something, hoping that he would close his mouth so that I didn't have to look at his manky teeth.

'I'm sorry, young lady, I seem to have missed what you said?' he replied, daring me to say it again.

'Well it's true,' I continued. 'We have to be here at half eight in the morning through until well after three in the afternoon, which is a long time. Therefore, lunch is a basic human right . . .' I paused for effect, realizing that I was going to be joining Jit and Dean in Herbert's office. '. . . And you're denying that right to my friends.'

'Well perhaps you'd like to complain to the European Court, Grace Parkhurst. Until then you can join your fellow idiots in my office. *MOVE!*'

I stood up and grinned at Jit before answering.

'There's no need to be so rude, is there?' I said, following the lads out of the dinner hall.

We had History straight after lunch, but by the time Herbert had finished with us we were late. I made all the excuses to Mr Woods, our teacher, who just ushered us in and told us to sit down. We were studying Britain's Roman history and halfway through the lesson Dean leaned over and whispered to me.

'There's a way out of having to eat late lunches,' he said.

'I'm *trying* to listen,' I told him, hoping that Mr Woods wouldn't see us talking. Getting into trouble once in a year was enough for me, never mind twice in one day.

'There's these things called socials,' continued Dean.

Jit, who was sitting on my other side, asked me what Dean was saying.

I elbowed Dean and told Jit to be quiet, as Mr Woods talked about something called the Fosse Way.

'What's he on about?' whispered Jit, a little too loudly.

'The Fosse Way, Jit,' said Mr Woods. 'Perhaps you have something to share?'

'Nossir,' replied Jit, pinching me on my thigh under the table.

'OWW!' I cried.

'Grace – what is going on?' asked Mr Woods.

'Nothing, sir. I got cramp . . .'

'Well stop it and pay attention . . .'

I gave Jit a death glare and returned to listening to Woods.

Dean kept quiet for maybe five minutes before he leaned over again.

'There's these socials . . .' he repeated.

'Shut up!' I whispered back.

'But . . .'

'Write it down,' I hissed, making a note of something that Mr Woods had just said.

Dean scribbled something in his pad and ripped it out quietly, folding it and passing it over. I waited until Mr Woods walked over to the windows before opening the note under the desk. I made out the words '*social*' and '*early lunch*'. I put it on my A4 pad and wrote '*what are you banging on about?*' underneath Dean's message, folded it and gave it back.

Jit leaned across me to see what was going on.

'Will you three please pay attention!' said Mr Woods, raising his voice, something that he rarely did.

'Sorry, sir,' I replied, going red in the face.

Woods carried on with his lecture as Dean read my reply. He started to write another message but I elbowed him again and shook my head. 'I'm not interested,' I whispered, ignoring him for the rest of the lesson. I couldn't work out his obsession with lunches. He was doing my head in.

Jit came back to my house after school and we sat in the cellar watching telly and drinking orange juice, freshly squeezed by my dad. Jit was moaning about the bits in it, telling me that it wasn't like the stuff that you got from Asda that came out of a carton.

'It's fresh,' I told him, not wanting to push it

because my parents could afford to buy fresh food everyday and Jit's mum couldn't.

'But the bits get stuck in your teeth!'

'I can get you some dental floss if you like. Or a toothpick . . .?'

Jit put his glass down and got up, walking over to the pool table. He started racking the balls.

'What were you and Dean talking about in History?' he asked, looking for the cue.

'Nothing really.'

'Didn't look like nothing,' he said, breaking off. 'You playin'?'

'With Dean?' I said, smiling. I knew that he was talking about pool but I just couldn't resist the wind-up.

Jit gave me a weird look as I got up and joined him at the table.

'He was trying to tell me about some idea he's got – how to get out of late lunches. I dunno what's got into him,' I said.

'He gets a bit funny sometimes,' replied Jit, before missing an easy shot.

I grabbed the cue and shoved Jit out of my way.

'You're rubbish . . . Here, let me show you how to play.'

I potted three balls before it was Jit's turn again.

'Yeah well, I'd be like the king of pool if I had one of these in my house,' he said, missing again.

'See? Rubbish!'

'So do you like . . . fancy him?' asked Jit, casually, not looking at me as he gave me the cue.

'Who?' I asked vaguely, playing dumb.

'Dean . . .'

'No. He's not my type.'

Jit looked puzzled.

'Why?' he asked me.

'Because he's a stinky boy – that's why.'

'Don't you like boys?'

'Yeah – just not Dean. Not like that anyway.'

'So who *do* you like?' he said, going a bit red.

'Dunno,' I replied, honestly. 'I've never really thought about it, Jit.'

'Oh . . .'

There was a knock at the door and then Hannah appeared at the foot of the stairs.

'Hey!'

'Hi, Han – wanna watch me beat Jit at pool?'

Hannah grinned and sat down, picking up my glass of juice without asking, and drinking from it.

'URRGH! This has got bits in it,' she said.

'I told her that,' said Jit, obviously happy not to continue our earlier conversation. Strange boy.

'It's fresh,' I repeated. 'It's supposed to be like that.'

'Oh shut up and take your shot, fancy pants,' grinned Hannah.

Stinky gimps . . .

FOUR

My mum got in from work around half past six and by that point Hannah and Jit had been invited to stay for dinner by my dad, who had appeared in the cellar doorway wearing beige cords, a green shirt and sandals, with an apron wrapped around his middle. He told us that he was making vegetarian sausages with ratatouille. I thought Jit would turn his nose up at that but he was too busy smirking at my dad's embarrassing dress sense to actually hear what he was saying. By the time my mum had sat down at the table and made her regular joke about opening a soup kitchen for the waifs and strays that I seemed to bring home from school, Jit had no choice but to eat the food in front of him.

'How is it, Jit?' my dad asked him. '"*Kickin*" or "*stink*," as you people say these days?'

'*Dad!*' I said, cringing.

'Relax, Grace – just because I've a few more years than you doesn't mean—'

'I think you'll find it does, Michael,' interrupted my mum with an amused look on her face.

'I think you're quite cool, Mr Parkhurst,' said Hannah, managing to keep a straight face.

'Yeah, the food's . . . er . . . cool, man,' added Jit.

'Wonderful,' smiled my dad, beaming, completely ignorant of the fact that everyone was having a laugh at his expense.

My mum asked Hannah how school was going.

'It's OK, Mrs Parkhurst – they still won't let me do a school newspaper though.'

'You and your school paper – that's all you ever chat about,' said Jit, picking at the food with his fork.

'I'm sure it would be quite a good idea,' replied my mum, before Hannah could swear at Jit.

'Yeah,' I added. 'We could write a gossip column and do news reports on everyone.'

'*And* voice *our* opinions about what the teachers make us do,' said Hannah. 'Like in a proper democracy!'

'What's that then, Professor Hannah, a new dance or something?' laughed Jit.

'Democracy is a system of government by the people within which—' began my dad, really seriously.

'I kinda know what it is, Mr Parkhurst,' admitted Jit, with a grin.

'I think you're becoming the butt of yet another joke,' my mum told Dad with a smile.

'I *knew* that,' he pretended.

He was good at pretending that he knew things. He had this theory that it was better to know a little bit about a lot than to know a lot about not very much. My mum called it the cow poo argument. As in he was talking cow poo.

'Anyway,' continued Hannah, ignoring Jit, 'if the teachers and the governors and everyone else get to tell us what to do, then we should have a right to tell them what we think of it. I mean it's not like I'm asking for longer holidays or half the day off.'

'It's a very valid point,' agreed my mum. 'What do you think, Grace?'

'Well I suppose it would be good, and I do think we should be allowed to tell the teachers what we think.'

'I'm very surprised at Mr Black,' said my mum. 'You would think that he might jump at something else to shout about on local radio.'

'I was online yesterday,' added Hannah, 'and in Birmingham they've got this Young People's Parliament thing, and we can't even get a paper going.'

Jit groaned.

'Do we have to talk about the stupid newspaper?'

'Why – was there something else you wanted to talk about?' asked my dad.

'Nah – it's just that in my house we just eat and watch the telly and that. I ain't used to all this *deep* conversation bit.'

My mum looked at me and then at Hannah.

'Is your mum on the same shift as Hannah's mum again?' she asked Jit.

'Er . . . yeah,' he said, really quickly. 'I've finished . . . can I go back down into the cellar?'

'Of course you can,' Mum said, and smiled.

'Thank you for dinner, Mr Parkhurst,' mumbled Jit, looking embarrassed, before he bolted out of his chair and down to the cellar.

I waited until he'd gone before speaking.

'He's a bit shy sometimes,' I said.

'He'll talk when he's ready,' replied my mum, the voice of experience. 'Boys are different to girls at this age.'

'He's just a weirdo,' grinned Hannah. 'Been like that since he was five!'

Everyone laughed, lightening the mood a bit, and then Mum started to clear up the plates.

'Grace, could you load these things into the dishwasher for me?' she said.

'OK. And then can I take my bike and walk Hannah and Jit home? I'll ride straight back.'

'Fine, but take your mobile with you just in case.'

We walked back about half an hour later. Well, I *wobbled* along on my bike and the other two walked. The route took us past a row of shops and through an alleyway where two lads had written some pointless graffiti on the fence: *'Bali and Parmy – Safe!'* – nothing else. No artwork or clever stuff. Just that. Silly people. At the end of the alley I asked why he didn't like talking about stuff at home. He gave me a funny look, shrugged, and then changed the subject.

'Your dad's funny,' he said, smiling. 'I don't mean funny bad – funny as in good. He makes me laugh and that.'

'Yeah, he's embarrassing,' I replied.

Hannah gave Jit a look.

'You're weird, Jit,' she told him.

'I ain't . . .'

'Yeah you are. Grace asked you a question about you and you turned it round and started talking about her dad – if that isn't weird I dunno what is,' she continued.

'I ain't got nothing to say – that's all,' he replied, looking sheepish.

'You know that you can talk to us if there's something wrong,' I added.

Jit glared at me.

'*What makes you think . . . ?* Never mind. Forget it. I just don't talk like you girls do.'

'But you could. If you wanted to . . .' I said again.

'Only I don't, so let's just leave it at that, man,' he replied, looking away.

'You're a weirdo,' said Hannah, smiling.

'Yeah, yeah,' said Jit, dismissively, as we rounded another corner and walked up to the crossroads where I was going to turn back.

Something shot past us, over the tops of our heads. A stone. It bounced off the roof of a car in front of us.

'What the . . . ?'

'Let's see how tough you are now, bruv!' came a shout from behind us.

We turned together to see Jason Patel and two of his friends behind us. Jit tensed up immediately and clenched his fists. I looked at Hannah who just shrugged. Then another stone flew right past her head and she went mad, shouting at Jason and his mates.

'Who you throwin' stones at?'

They rode up on their bikes and started to circle us. Jason kicked out at Jit and then they started laughing. Jit was going red and I started to get scared. Hannah stood where she was, her eyes blazing.

'Oh *yeah* – you're bad boys, you are!' she told them.

'Badder than you,' said Jason, kicking out at Jit again.

'*Get lost!*' shouted Jit, watching Jason as he came round again.

'See how you got your girlfriends to back you up?' Jason said, laughing.

He went to kick Jit again, only this time Jit grabbed his leg and yanked him off his bike. Jason went flying, ending up in a tangle with the frame. The other two lads got off their bikes and grabbed Jit, shoving him around. And then I heard a car horn beeping. The car stopped and Mr Singh, a sports teacher at school, jumped out, still wearing his tracksuit. '*What the hell do you think you're doing?*' he shouted at Jason and his mates.

The two lads that had hold of Jit let him go, grabbed their bikes and rode off. Jason tried to follow them but Mr Singh grabbed him.

'*Gerroff me!*' shouted Jason.

'What do you think you're doing?' demanded Mr Singh.

'I'll tell my dad,' squealed Jason. 'He'll get the police onto you!'

Mr Singh let go of Jason and shrugged.

'Call them right now,' he told Jason, holding out his own mobile.

'Tosser!' said Jason, grabbing his bike.

'Ain't so tough now!' Hannah said, laughing.

Jason glared at Jit.

'See *you* tomorrow,' he said with a sneer, before riding off after his mates.

Mr Singh asked us if we were OK before telling Jit and Hannah that he would drive them home. Jit tried to put on a bad boy act and said that he'd be fine, but Mr Singh insisted and Jit eventually agreed.

'How about you, Grace?' Mr Singh asked me.

'I'll be OK. I've got my bike and I only live round the corner,' I said, feeling a little less scared.

'OK then, but go straight home and if you get any more trouble from that lot – you tell me,' he said, talking to all of us.

'See you in the morning,' said Hannah.

'Yeah,' I replied, looking at Jit. 'You OK, Jit?'

'Yeah . . . see you later, Grace.'

I got on my bike and rode home, wondering whether Jason would have a go at Jit in school the next day. When I got in, my mum saw that my face was red and asked me if I was all right.

'Yeah,' I told her. 'Just rode back too quickly.'

FIVE

Mr Black was waiting at the school gates the next morning, as usual, but he was in such a good mood that he forgot to tell us off. He said something about the birds singing and it being a beautiful day and ushered us in.

As we walked to our form room I wondered whether to bring up what had happened the evening before. But Jit was busy teasing Dean about a spot on his nose.

'Must be hard having that thing stuck to the end of your nose – must interfere with your sight,' he said, as Dean told him to get lost for about the fiftieth time.

'Ah – don't be arsey about it – we've all had 'em,' teased Jit. 'Ain't that right, Grace?'

'What?' I asked as we walked into our form room and Mrs Dooher looked up from her desk, shaking her head at us.

'*Spots*,' replied Jit, lowering his voice. 'We've all had spots.'

'Stop winding Dean up, Jit,' I told him, taking a seat next to Hannah, who was doodling on a notepad. Jit ignored me.

'Thing's got a life of its own. It's so big it's probably got its own atmosphere!' he continued.

Dean kissed his teeth at Jit and turned his back on him.

'Like a planet sitting on the end of your conk – your own likkle planet!'

'And you can talk 'bout conks?' Hannah told Jit, winking at me.

'What?' asked Jit, screwing up his face.

'If I had a nose the size of yours I wouldn't be laughing at no one else.'

Jit went red and shut up.

'See dat, man! You soon hush up when you get dissed!' laughed Dean, ruffling Jit's hair.

'Gerroff!'

'Calm down now, form,' interrupted Mrs Dooher, standing up and facing us all.

'*Calm down! Calm down!*' mimicked a lad called Raj from behind us, pretending to be a Scouser. Mrs

Dooher gave him a dirty look before she continued.

'Excuse the comedian at the back, form. Right, some of you may have noticed that our esteemed principal, Mr Black, is in a good mood this morning . . .'

'Man acted like he was off his head on something when we come in,' replied Jit.

'. . . *Came* in, Jit. You *came* in,' corrected Mrs Dooher.

'Whatever . . .'

'Well there's a good reason for Mr Black's mood. The school has just been given funding to rebuild the library and turn the old, disused block into a media and languages centre!'

The disused block was round the back of the school and had been empty for years. Some of the pupils said it was haunted, but according to my dad it was just an old Victorian building that was going to ruin. At my first ever parents' evening at the school he had proceeded to tell Mr Black what a shame that was, before offering to buy it and do it up. Strange man.

The rest of the form '*oohed*' and '*ahhed*' at the mention of new funding and Mrs Dooher went on to explain that the work would start in the next few months, meaning that the new building would be ready by the following school year. Pushpa, one of the girls, gave everyone a letter for their parents, outlining the plans. When she got to Jit, he blew her a kiss and she turned bright red, running off to her seat, where her friends began to tease her.

'You flirt,' I said to him.

'You jealous?' he asked me, smiling.

'You wish, stinky boy!'

It was meant as a joke but Jit gave me a funny look before pouting and turning his attention back to Dean's zit. This time Suky and Imtiaz told Jit to stop.

'You lot are boring!' said Jit.

'Act your age for a change,' added Imtiaz.

'Like you act yours, you mean? *Sixty* . . .?'

'Will you little beggars shut up!' shouted Mrs Dooher. Well actually, it was more like she raised her voice because she was far too lovely to shout. And even in raising her voice she broke into a smile.

'You're rubbish at tellin' us off, miss,' laughed Dean.

'Ooh you cheeky little . . .'

'Just tell him to take his zit and get lost!' shouted Jit.

'Why don't you—?' began Dean.

'All right, all right, lads,' said Mrs Dooher calming

them down. 'Off you all go to your lessons and don't forget that the music room is being painted and is out of bounds for a few days.'

The rest of what she said got lost in the din as the form scraped back their chairs and went off to lessons. I followed Hannah out of the classroom, with Imi and Suky. Behind us, Mrs Dooher called out to Dean and as he went to speak to her she handed him a note. He opened it, read it and then stuffed it into one of his trouser pockets, grinning to himself.

I'm often told that I'm too nosy, always wanting to know what's going on, so I tried really hard not to wonder about what was in the note. It didn't work though. By the time we got to Science, I would have given him my lunch money to find out what it said. Only he wouldn't say, telling me to shut up and pay attention. And when I tried to get Jit to join in with my nosing, all I got was a funny look and a shrug. Boys . . .

At break we stood around by the tennis courts to one side of the main school building. The courts were full of boys playing football and running around yelling at each other. Groups of girls stood and watched them, staring at the ones that they fancied. Hannah was talking about an article that she'd read in a newspaper about exactly which bugs hid in which type of meat. She was telling us about how dirty chickens were and how they had some kind of organism living in their bottoms when Jit swore. I stopped listening to Hannah and gave Jit a funny look.

'Jason Patel,' he said, nodding towards the lower tennis court.

'Raas!' said Dean, whatever that meant.

Jason and two of his goons were walking over, all scary looking.

Instinctively I looked around for a teacher. There were two of them, Mr Singh, and a young English teacher called Miss Khan, standing by the entrance to the school, holding mugs of coffee. If I hadn't been so preoccupied with Jason I would have pointed out to Hannah that Mr Singh and Miss Khan seemed to be flirting with each other, only I was scared, so I told Hannah that I was going to tell them about Jason. She nodded and said that she'd wait with Jit and Dean. I was walking over to Mr Singh when I heard the shouting start.

'*FIGHT! FIGHT! FIGHT!*'

Groups of people gathered around as Jason swore at Jit and Dean, calling them 'grasses'. Hannah tried to intervene but one of Jason's mates shoved her to one side and then Jason and Jit started to have a scrap. Lots of the younger lads were egging them on and then I heard a whistle. It was Mr Singh, sprinting over to the commotion. Behind him, three more male teachers came running out of school. I turned back to the fight and saw Dean punch one of Jason's friends. Jit was on the floor with Jason kneeling on his chest, punching him in the face.

Mr Singh grabbed Jason and held him whilst the other teachers took hold of Dean, Jit and Jason's friends, who were all swearing at each other. Yet more teachers ran out and told the rest of us to get inside. I started to walk away with Hannah when Mr Singh called us back.

'You two were there yesterday so I'd like you to stay and help sort this mess out,' he said, letting Mr Woods and the other teachers take Jason and his mates to Mr Black's office.

'But I don't know why . . .' I began.

'I still need to talk to you, Grace,' said Mr Singh.

Dean and Jit were standing next to him. Jit had a

swollen eye, which he kept on touching. He looked really angry.

'*Well?*' asked Mr Singh as Hannah and me joined the lads.

'Well what?' replied Dean, angrily.

'Yesterday I had to stop a fight between Jit and Jason and now, today, I've had to do the same thing. What's going on?'

'Ask dem, man,' said Dean. 'It's my boy standing here with a bust-up eye.'

'I'm asking *you*, Dean,' Mr Singh told him.

'Jason just picked on them,' said Hannah. 'It's not their fault that he's a bully . . .'

'Is that what it is, Jit? Jason's bullying you?'

Jit gave Hannah a death stare and then shrugged.

'It's nuttin',' he told Mr Singh.

'It's obviously more than nothing, son. I know that you didn't start it. But I need you to report Jason. That way Mr Black can take some kind of action.'

'Sack that – me nah grass up no one!' said Jit, defiantly.

'An' nuh bother even ask *me*,' added Dean.

Hannah shook her head at them.

'It's not grassin',' she said.

'Yeah – it's not . . .' I agreed, only for Jit and Dean to shoot me a look each. Looks that said shut up.

'We need to do something. This isn't the first time – Jason's already on a warning,' said Mr Singh.

'It's nuttin',' repeated Jit, sullenly.

'Look – you two are no good to the football team if you've been beaten up,' said Mr Singh, trying a different tack, but the lads just ignored him, and looked at the floor.

'Fine . . . but this will get out of hand unless something is done,' said Mr Singh. 'Now, get to your next lesson and remember, if anything like this happens again, tell me.'

Hannah led the way back into school, her eyes blazing with anger at Jit and Dean.

'You two are so messed up.'

'What do you know about it?' asked Jit, touching his eye again.

'You gonna let Jason get away with it? He's a bully.'

'We'll deal with him our way,' replied Dean.

'Yeah – because you're so *bad*,' sneered Hannah.

Jit ignored her and asked me what the next lesson was.

'Maths,' I said, smiling at him, hoping that he would calm down.

'Sack that – I'm not going,' he said, walking off in the other direction.

'*Jit!*' I called out after him.

'Leave him, Grace,' said Hannah. 'He'll be OK in a while.'

'But he'll get into trouble,' I said, really concerned.

'Trouble follows him around,' said Dean. 'He's used to it.'

We walked into our classroom and sat down. Mrs Lee-Cross, the Maths teacher, asked us why we were late.

'They was fightin', miss!' someone shouted out.

'And where's Jit?' she asked us.

As Dean and Hannah shrugged and sat down, I waited for one of them to say something. When they didn't, I did.

'He's got a black eye, miss. I think he's with Mr Singh.'

'Oh – thank you, Grace. Now let's get down to mathematics . . .'

SIX

The lesson was boring but then again it was Maths. It was one of those things that I just didn't like no matter how hard I tried. My dad had taken to giving me extra tuition at home, only his tuition was about as useful as an eighty-year-old in a boy band. We were constantly interrupted by phone calls from his clients, too. Not that I ever complained. It was lovely of him to try in the first place. In the end my mum twigged that I wasn't doing as well as I could and she got me maths tutor software for my computer. It's still in the box, wrapped in its Cellophane, gathering dust in the no-go zone under my bed. With all the other fun things that you can do with a PC, like chatting to people on the net and instant messaging, why would I want to use it to learn boring, stinky maths?

But it wasn't just the lesson; I was worried about Jit too, wondering where he had gone. Mr Black stalked the corridors of Devana High like a security guard during lessons, on the lookout for skiving pupils and 'unwanted visitors', as he liked to call them. A year before we had got to the school, there had been an incident in which a pervy bloke had walked into the school and locked himself in the girls' toilets. It was in the papers and on the local TV news, and the school had tightened security because of it. Hence Mr Black's walkabouts.

I was busy thinking of good places to hide in if you were going to skive a lesson, when Mrs Lee-Cross told some of the pupils that they could go. I looked at my watch. It was ten to twelve. Four lads got up, all from the same table and walked to the door. And then Dean scraped back his chair and joined them. I looked up at him, wondering where he was going.

Imtiaz nudged me.

'Where's he off to?' he whispered.

'Dunno,' I replied.

'He's trying it on, I reckon,' said Suky, leaning across the table.

Mrs Lee-Cross gave Dean a raised eyebrow and then continued to talk about some maths problem or other,

as I sat with my mouth open and watched him walk
out with the gang of nerds.

'Well, he got away with it,' whispered Imtiaz.

'Maybe he's gone to find Jit,' added Hannah.

'Yeah, that'll be it,' I agreed.

'Are you three listening to *me* or having your own
conversation?' asked Mrs Lee-Cross over the heads of
the other pupils.

'Listening to you, miss,' replied Imtiaz. 'Honest . . .'

'Good, then perhaps one of your table would care
to work out the problem I've just been outlining . . .
Grace, why don't you tell us the solution?'

I sat there, conscious that my face was turning
redder by the second. I could hear Imtiaz sniggering as
I '*ummed*' and '*aahed*'.

'Er . . . well, miss . . .' I began, wishing that I'd paid
attention.

I didn't see Dean all lunch time and Jit only surfaced
about ten minutes before we were due at afternoon
registration, with a purple bruise around his eye and a
face like thunder. The rest of us were finishing up our
lunches in the dining hall, discussing ways to convince

Mr Black that we needed a school newspaper. Imtiaz saw Jit coming first.

'Here's a story for it . . . "*Boy Gets Given Black Eye*" . . .' he said, as we turned to Jit.

'You OK?' asked Suky, getting up and putting her arm around him.

'Do I look like I'm OK?' snapped Jit.

Suky pulled back from him, hurt, and his face softened a bit.

'Sorry,' he said, surprising all of us. It was a word that he didn't use very often.

'It's no problem, Jit,' smiled Suky, with a sisterly concern in her eyes.

'You should have told Singhy what happened,' said Imtiaz.

'Yeah – but then Jason would have got into even more trouble.'

'*So?* That's his problem,' replied Imtiaz.

'And mine the next time I see him out on the street – 's'all right for you . . . he lives near me.'

'Yeah but he ain't that tough,' said Imtiaz. 'And anyway, if he touches you outside school you can have him done for assault or something.'

Jit shook his head and looked at Hannah. 'Don't

work that way, bro,' he said. 'It always comes back to you. If it ain't him, it's his mates.'

'Man, you make it sound like you live in Iraq or somewhere like that. It's not that bad.'

'Yeah but it's a different place to where you live, Imi,' added Hannah, in support of Jit.

'Whatever . . .' replied Imtiaz.

I could feel an argument coming so I decided to do my usual and change the subject.

'Where do you think Dean's got to?' I asked.

Jit gave me another of his looks. 'What's up with Dean?' he asked, looking a bit concerned, as though maybe Dean had got into more trouble with Jason Patel.

'He got out of Maths early – same time as the nerds – and Little Miss Won't-Mind-My-Own is wondering why,' said Hannah.

'Well – at least I'm honest,' I replied, defending myself. 'And anyway, if you're going to be a journalist *you'll* have to develop a nosy streak too.'

'I thought he'd gone looking for you, Jit,' said Suky, stabbing at her food with a fork.

'You don't have to kill that you know – thing dead already,' replied Jit, pointing at the mush on her plate.

'Just checking . . .' she replied, smiling.

Mr Black's voice bellowed around the hall, telling us to leave. '*Come along, Devana High – it's time for the dinner staff to clear up now that you've had your lunches . . . It's only . . .*'

'Fair . . .' mimicked Suky.

We got up to leave, taking our trays to the counter. Hannah and Suky walked off ahead with Imtiaz, in a hurry to get to English, which they loved. I hung back with Jit.

'So Dean didn't try to find you?' I asked.

'You seem really interested in Dean lately,' he snapped. But then he looked like he regretted what he'd said.

'I am,' I said, teasing.

'Oh . . .'

I decided to change the subject quickly before the silly boy got upset. I *was* only teasing . . .

'So where *were* you all lesson?' I asked him.

'In the toilets . . .'

'The boys'?' I asked stupidly.

'Well I'm not gonna hide in the *girls'* toilets am I?' he grinned.

'Doesn't Mr Black check them?'

'Yeah but the one time he came in I pretended I was using it.'

'So you spent an *hour* in the *loo*?' I replied, disgusted at the idea.

'Locked in a cubicle, yeah,' Jit said, as we made our way to English.

'You *stinky, stinky* boy!'

'Shut up, Grace . . .'

Dean ignored all my efforts to find out where he had been all afternoon, telling me that it was personal and I had no right to know. Only he said it with a grin, so that I'd know he was winding me up. Which would only wind me up even more. Which, I *suppose*, was the whole point.

By the time we were walking down to get the bus I was offering Dean my iPod for a week, on loan, if only he'd tell me where he'd been. He continued to say 'no'. Eventually, though, he grabbed my hand and pulled me to one side, out of earshot of the others.

'I'll come round later and tell you,' he said. 'But only if you promise that you'll keep it a secret.'

I promised.

'I'll come by about seven-ish then,' added Dean.

'Cool,' I said, looking towards the rest of our friends and seeing Jit staring back at me.

I thought about asking Dean if we could let Jit in on the secret but realized that it might be amusing not to, for a few days at least. Not to be mean, or anything. Just to wind him up a bit. I started wishing time away as the bus crawled through the traffic, excited that I was about to share a secret with Dean. I loved secrets – they were so much fun . . .

SEVEN

I heard the phone ringing upstairs as Dean placed some pool balls in a row for the sixth time and attempted to show me what he called his 'killer' shot.

'See how the balls is all lined up and that? Well – if I hit the one at the end with the white ball then the one at the *other* end will double into that pocket there.' He pointed at one of the corner pockets.

'You said that last time and it didn't work. And the time before that,' I teased. 'Will it *ever* work, Dean?'

Dean gave me a withering look.

'GRACE!' shouted my dad from the top of the stairs. 'PHONE . . . !'

'You practise your shot, sonny, and I'll go see who's on the phone,' I told Dean, as he squinted at the balls.

I ran upstairs into the hallway and picked up the handset.

'Hello?'

'*Hi, Grace . . . it's . . . er . . . me. What you doin'?*'

It was Jit.

'Not a lot . . . Dean's come over and he's showing me some pool shot or other.'

'*Dean? Oh . . . can I . . . ?*'

'You always do anyway,' I replied.

'*See you in a bit then . . . ?*' he asked, rather than said, which was unlike him.

'OK then, you weirdo . . . can you stop by the shop and get me some Maltesers?'

'*Er . . . yeah. If I can get some dough . . . I haven't . . .*'

'That's OK – I'll nip out and get some myself,' I said quickly, hoping that I hadn't embarrassed him.

'*Cool.*'

The line went dead. I put the handset down and went back to the cellar where Dean was lining up his shot yet again.

'Are you going to get that right or are we gonna be here all night?' I said, smiling, as I sank into an armchair.

'Patience . . . you're watching an artist at work y'know,' replied Dean, taking the shot.

The ball that was supposed to end up in a pocket glanced off a cushion, missing by about three inches.

'So is that your secret then, Dean – that you can't play pool?' I asked, impatient for him to tell me about where he'd been earlier.

'I keep telling you, Grace. You ain't funny so don't bother wastin' your time.'

'Well if you're not going to tell me . . .'

'Who was on the phone?' he asked, changing the subject.

'Jit – he's on his way round so you'd better tell me quickly otherwise I'll tell him that you're keeping secrets.'

'*Ehh* check you out . . . Little Miss Blackmail!'

I laughed and told him to shut up and tell me.

'Well it's like this, and I told you about this before, only you was too dumb to listen. I joined a social . . .'

'What?' I replied.

'A social. A lunch time activity club. That way, even when I'm on late lunches, every Wednesday I get to leave Maths early and get a nice hot dinner instead of that concrete they keep for the late lunches.' Dean came and sat down on the sofa, pleased with himself.

'You joined a *nerd* society?' I said, wondering if he'd gone mad.

'Yeah . . . Chess Club, innit? Why, what you sayin' – that I can't play chess if I want to?'

'You can play chess till your fingers drop off, you stinky boy,' I snorted. 'But I'm thinking that you didn't join to pick up tips on where the pawn goes.'

'Elementary, my dear Parkhurst . . . like my man Sherlock Holmes always says. I joined to get out of Maths early and to get a hot dinner.'

'So what did you do all lunch time – talk about chess with nerdy kids?' I asked, imagining the conversations that might possibly come up.

'Yeah well, they *tried* to talk to me but I just told 'em to go away,' said Dean.

'So you didn't actually get involved or anything?'

Dean sat forward excitedly. 'Nah, man! It's a blag, innit? All I did was show up, sit at the back and move a few pieces around a board.'

'So who's the teacher in charge of it then?'

'That Wilson – the *Science teacher*? The one that looks like he needs a hot meal?'

'The skinny man who mumbles to himself?'

I'd seen him in the corridors, walking around like a twig in a lab coat.

'Yeah – *Willy* Wilson . . . and he didn't even notice me. He just came in, spoke to a couple of the top nerds and then left.'

'So you had *no* supervision and no one *checked* to see if you were actually there for the chess?' I asked, amazed *and* interested.

'*Exactly*, Sister Gee,' he replied.

I smiled and told him to call me Sister Gee again. I liked it – it made me sound like a female MC. Dean laughed along and told me that I could join Chess Club if I wanted to.

'Anyone can join . . . it's just that most of the all right kids don't know about it. It's like a secret Harry Potter lookalike society . . . only for those in the know and that. You should have seen the looks on their faces when I showed up.'

'Can I register for it tomorrow?' I asked.

'Yeah – I just asked Miss Dooher about it and she gave me a list of activities . . .'

'There's no catch or anything?'

'Just two. *One* – you get to leave lessons before everyone else and *two* – you get to eat a nice hot dinner or, in your case, a sandwich that don't look like it's been farted on by an elephant.'

'Why would an elephant fart flatten my sandwich?' I asked, giggling.

'Oh you know what I mean,' said Dean. 'So what do you reckon then?'

'I'm up for it,' I said as the door to the cellar opened and my dad called down. 'Grace – Jit's here . . . I'll send him down.'

As Jit came down the stairs I quickly finished my conversation with Dean.

'Cool – let's do that tomorrow,' I said, turning to smile at Jit.

'Do what?' he asked, looking from me to Dean.

'Nuttin' man,' smiled Dean. 'Just something that Grace and me gonna do.'

'What – like *together* . . . ?'

'Yes,' I told Jit. 'But don't worry – we aren't getting married or anything.'

I smiled as Jit raised an eyebrow and came over all confused. He really was funny sometimes. He ignored me in the end and he and Dean played pool together as I watched telly. About an hour later Hannah came round with some homework and we tried to do that as the lads argued over free shots and stuff.

* * *

The next morning I signed up for the weekly Wednesday Chess Club and waited impatiently for the week to pass so that I could leave Maths early with Dean. I found Dean by the tennis courts at break, chatting up some girl.

'Done it!' I beamed at him, butting in on his conversation.

Dean told the girl that he would 'check for her' later and I asked what he was going to check her for. He grinned at me and told me to stop being so posh.

'You know,' he began, 'last night Jit was asking me about our secret all the way home, man.'

'Did you tell him?' I asked.

'Nah – let him sweat . . . I think he's got it wrong anyway. He probably thinks that you and me are going out or something . . .'

'URGH! No disrespect but you smell.'

'Hush up, man – me have a bath *every* day – twice 'pon a Saturday.'

We laughed as we walked over to the others, who were standing just inside the entrance to school. Jit gave us a strange look when he saw us and I realized that maybe Dean was right about Jit being suspicious.

EIGHT

The following Wednesday Dean and I got up to leave Mrs Lee-Cross' Maths lesson with the nerds. Jit was sitting beside me and asked me where I was going but Mrs Lee-Cross told him to mind his own business and concentrate on maths. He shrugged and asked me to tell him later. I smiled and followed Dean out of the room, aware of the funny looks that Hannah, Suky and Imi were giving us too. I so loved having a secret.

We went down to the dinner hall and I was amazed at the fresh-looking sandwiches laid out in front of me, all lovely and edible-looking. We were the first to get there and by the time the lunch bell rang, we were already eating ours.

'Come on,' said Dean, wolfing down some of his chips and wrapping the rest in a piece of bread, 'bring the rest with you. We don't want the others to see us and they're on first lunch.'

He got up to take his tray to the counter.

'Oh yeah – nearly forgot,' I said, grabbing the remains of my sandwich and my apple and heading off after him.

We took a long route to the science block, so that we would avoid the others as they came in for lunch. Some of the other pupils from Chess Club were already there when we arrived, concentrating hard on their next moves. Dean mouthed the word 'sad' at me as we took a table at the back of the room, by the window. He unfolded the chess board in front of us, taking the pieces out of their box.

'I don't even know where these things are supposed to go,' he said, smiling like a nutter.

'I've played before,' I admitted, rearranging the pieces so that they were on the correct squares.

'I should've guessed!' he told me. 'Grace Parkhurst – used to be a nerd but she all right now!'

'Get stuffed!' I replied, embarrassed.

'Nah – it's OK. Looks like an interestin' kinda game.'

'Don't laugh at me or I'll tell the others,' I warned.

'Oh yeah – er . . . sorry.'

I grinned and moved my first pawn. Dean looked at me like I was crazy.

'What you *doing* Grace? We ain't gonna actually *play* the game,' he said.

'We can pretend . . . that way we can have a chat and not look like we're just here to miss part of Maths and get an early lunch.'

'Yeah but that's why we are here,' replied Dean.

'*Ah* – but *they* don't know that, do they?' I told him, nodding at the rest of the Chess Club, which was being supervised by Mr Wilson.

He looked over at us and smiled shyly. I grinned back and, raising my voice, told him that I absolutely adored chess. Dean kicked me under the table.

'Grace!' he whispered, giving me a filthy look, as Mr Wilson tottered over on his twiglet legs.

'And you are . . . ?' asked Wilson.

'Grace Parkhurst,' I beamed. 'And this is my friend Dean Chambers.'

'Well, hello and welcome to the Chess Club, people,' grinned Wilson, trying to act cool but sounding like my dad.

'It's a really *cool* club. We've got a club challenge and a couple of videos about opening gambits and master tactics and next month we're entering the top two players in a challenge with another school. That'll be fun!'

Dean was looking at Wilson like he was crazy.

'Yeah,' he replied, 'the Chess Club sounds bad!'

Wilson smiled at us as I struggled to hold down my giggles. I shot up and ran to the loo, not coming back until I'd cried with laughter, by which time Wilson had gone and Dean was busy rolling up bits of paper and flicking them at a lad called Wesley Magoogan who was good at anything that involved numbers but bad at everything else. Wesley was ignoring the paper bullets that were constantly landing on his board. He was far too busy trying to beat his chess partner, Robert Sargeant. Robert was just removing the paper as it landed, without even looking up at Dean.

'Dean – don't be such a bully,' I said.

'I'm only playing,' he protested.

'Yeah but if they complain to Wilson he'll kick us out and bang goes our little scam,' I pointed out.

'Good thinking, Sister Gee – I'll stop.'

'So what do we do now then?' I asked.

'Let's write a rap,' said Dean, excitedly.

'A *rap*?'

'Yeah – you know – lyrics dat flow in a way dat you *know* will get the gal dem fe *crow*!' said Dean without taking a breath.

'But I've never written a—'

'Come, Sister Gee! I ain't gonna let you keep the name otherwise.'

I smiled and pulled a pad and a pen from my bag.

'But what if Wilson comes back?' I asked, as Dean grabbed my stationery.

'We'll just tell him that we're writing down the moves and that – to learn them.'

'Oh go on then,' I said, trying to think of words that rhymed.

'Right – we need a topic to write about,' said Dean, doodling on a page of paper.

'What about the Chess Club?' I suggested.

'Nah – that's lame. What about something to do with school though – like Mr Herbert?'

'Mr Herbert? What could we possibly rap about him?' I asked.

Dean thought about it for a moment before replying.

'Dunno – what about his spots or his ratty face?' he said.

'Or the way he goes red in the face when he shouts?' I added, warming to the task.

'Yeah, man!' shouted Dean, alerting the rest of the Chess Club.

'Ssh . . .!' came a joint whisper from the rest of the Chess Club.

'Hush yuh mout', man!' replied Dean, harshly.

The rest of the club turned back to their games, most of them red in the face.

'Dean!'

Dean gave me a shrug of his shoulders.

'What? They wanna mind them own, innit . . .'

'Ooh bad boy!' I replied, jokingly.

'Anyway like we was sayin' – Herbert . . .'

I was about to reply when Dean smiled suddenly and started to write some words down on the paper. Five minutes later he proudly pushed it in my direction, grinning from ear to ear. I picked it up and read the words that he'd written. I was amazed at how quickly he'd done it. 'Yuh see me?' he said, boasting. 'Me is the *Dan*!'

I finished reading it and looked at him.

'It's a bit lame, I reckon,' I said, teasing him.

His face dropped. 'What *you* know about it, anyway?' he said, kissing his teeth and dismissing me with a wave of his hand.

'Well – it's not like I can even rap.'

'Let me rap it to you – it's different to the way

it seems when it's written down,' he told me.

'You're going to rap *here* – in Chess Club?' I asked.

'Yeah – it ain't no big thing.'

Dean took the sheet of paper and stood up, clearing his throat and daring the rest of the club to tell him to shut up with one of his looks. They just sat where they were, bemused but interested all the same. Dean bowed and spoke . . . '*Yes, people! Right now for your entertainment and pleasure MC D-C ah go give you the Herbert Rap!*'

Most of the club giggled and looked at each other. Dean smiled at me and cleared his throat again.

> '*See, geezer sits in his chair,*
> *Shoutin' like he just don't care.*
> *But when him check out all the facts,*
> *Geezer's headin' fe a heart attack!*
>
> *So chill, Mr Teacher, chill out nuh man,*
> *Stop shouting at us, loud as you can.*
> *'Cos one day soon, and it's a fact,*
> *You ago give yourself a heart attack!*
> *Give yourself a heart attack!*

Wid yuh red-up face and the hair you lack,
Sometimes you even smell kinda wack.
So just chill out, geezer – give peace a try,
'Cos if you don't – you might just die . . .'

The rest of the club just sat where they were, grinning to each other, as Dean finished. I looked at him, smiled, and started to clap. One by one the nerds broke into laughter and clapped along, just as the afternoon registration bell rang. Dean grabbed his stuff and grinned like he'd won a prize or something. I got up, collected my things and followed him down to registration.

'Yeah, you were right,' I told him.

'See? Looks lame on paper but when you actually rap it . . .' Dean was saying, as we walked into the form room.

Mrs Dooher smiled at us and told us to have a sweet from a bag she had on her desk. Dean grinned, grabbed a sweet and then hugged Mrs Dooher.

'You is *soooo* lovely.' He gave her a kiss on her cheek. Mrs Dooher shook him off and went and sat down.

'You *little get!*' she said, smiling.

Jit walked in with the rest of the gang and they sat down.

'Where was you then?' he asked me.

'Nowhere,' I replied, trying to sound mysterious.

Jit shrugged his shoulders and turned away from me. 'Suit yourself,' he said, but not to my face.

All of a sudden I wasn't as pleased with myself. I'd upset him. '*Jit!*' I whispered, as Mrs Dooher read out some notices.

He didn't reply and when the bell went he shot out of the classroom before anyone else. Hannah noticed and shook her head as we followed the others to classes.

'He's not a happy bunny, is he?' she said.

'I think I upset him,' I told her.

'Nah – he's just immature,' replied Hannah.

'*No he's not!*' I half shouted.

I don't know why but Hannah's comment had made me want to defend Jit. It was so not me. I went red in the face. But only for a moment.

'Calm down, Grace,' Hannah said, smiling. 'Anyway – where *did* you and Dean get to over lunch time . . .?'

NINE

The others were asking me and Dean where we'd been every five minutes, for the rest of the day. In the evening I rang Jit, who told me that he was busy and couldn't come round, which was odd for him. I put it out of my mind until the next morning when he didn't turn up at the bus stop.

'Where's Jit?' I asked Dean as we got on the bus.

'Dunno.'

'Didn't you call for him?' I said, taking my ticket and following Dean upstairs, as the bus pulled away from the stop.

'Yeah – but no one answered the door. He's probably pretending to be ill or something.'

I looked down the road to see if he might be running late for the bus, but there was no sign of him – just an old couple walking their poodle and a gang of older lads, including Jason Patel, who were making no effort to catch the last bus that would get them to school on time. I wondered why so many of the pupils who lived near Dean and Jit walked the fifteen minute journey to the stop near my house. It didn't make any sense at all, but then they were all boys. Odd.

'I hope he's all right,' I told Dean, but he was busy taking something out of his bag.

'This is a list of all the other socials that you can go to,' he said, holding a folded sheet of A4 up.

'What, you mean we don't *have* to go to Chess Club on Wednesdays?' I asked, wondering what other delights were available.

'Nah, on Wednesdays Chess Club is the best one. These are for the rest of the week,' he replied, grinning.

'We can go to more than one lunch-time club?' I hadn't even considered that possibility.

'Well yeah – I *think* we can. I'm not sure that there's a limit or anything,' he said, acting a bit sly.

I took the piece of paper from him. On it was a box grid with the days of the week from Tuesday to Friday down one side and a list of the available clubs and activities against each day. At the top of the page, in bold type, was a note that said we were only allowed to attend two of these socials in any week. I held the note in front of Dean's face.

'You little liar. It says here that—'

Dean grinned even wider. 'That's the official rule but who's gonna check?' he asked me.

'Anyone. Mr Black or one of the other teachers. One of the other pupils even,' I pointed out.

'No one bothered to check us at the last one. There weren't no register taken was there?'

'Yes – but that doesn't mean another teacher won't take a register at one of the other socials,' I argued.

'Relax, Grace. It ain't no big deal. I'm sure that them nerds go to more than they're supposed to anyway.'

I gave him a raised eyebrow. Yeah, like Wesley Magoogan and his mates were going to break the rules. Dean kissed his teeth at me.

'OK then – let's ask them,' he said, looking round for a suitable candidate. He didn't find one. Pupils like Wesley and Robert Sargeant were already at school by the time we caught our bus each morning. They caught the earlier one. Dean shrugged.

'We'll ask that Wesley later,' he said, 'and anyway – we can pick *one* more . . .'

I looked at the list of clubs and the days they were available. Dean leaned over and pointed at the list for Thursdays.

'Thursdays we have English with Herbert, right?' So if we pick one for that day we can get out of his lesson ten minutes early – that'll wind him right up.' He sat back and smiled at me.

'But he'll get suspicious,' I said.

'He can't do *jack* though, can he? We're *allowed* to go to these things.'

'I dunno,' I said, 'I can see this ending in tears.'

'Grace – you sound like your dad. Leave it out. It's just a blag.'

'OK – so which one should we pick?' I asked, looking at the list.

Dean's grin stayed where it was, like he'd fallen victim to that thing your parents tell you when you're young about the wind changing direction and your face staying that way.

'I took the liberty,' he said, in what he would probably call a posh voice, 'of choosing for you, m'dear.'

I gave him a look. 'I'm sorry?'

'I chose one for you already,' he repeated.

'*Dean!*'

76

'*Well* – I knew you'd be OK about it once I'd *told* you so I picked one for you. *Us* even.'

'Which one?' I asked, praying that he hadn't picked Science Club or Model Making, which were both on the list.

'Er . . . Science . . .'

'*Dean!*' I shouted, and the whole top deck of the bus looked at us. Someone wolf whistled and shouted that we were having a lovers' tiff. I stuck my fingers up at them. Dean cracked up.

'Only kidding, Sister Gee, man. I picked the Book Club. We start today . . .'

I was about to say something but I stopped myself and thought about it. We were going to miss ten minutes of English every Thursday to go to a book club. Even Mr Herbert couldn't complain about that. And I love books. I might even enjoy it.

'OK – that's a good choice,' I said, smiling. '*But* you never read anything.'

'I can start, can't I?' replied Dean. 'And anyways, it's a *blag*, Grace. A *blag* . . .'

Jit hadn't turned up at school either but Hannah had a note from his mum saying that he was ill. I would have worried about him if Hannah hadn't produced the note, but I was happy that he was ill. *Well*, not happy exactly, but relieved that it wasn't something else – like he was upset or in trouble with someone. Dean and me went looking for Wesley and found him by the stairs that led up to the science block, waiting for his friends.

When Dean called out Wesley's name he went red and froze to the spot.

'Relax, Wesley,' smiled Dean, 'I just want some advice, bro.'

Wesley's face slowly changed from beetroot to strawberry.

'What can I help you with . . . er . . . Dean?' he managed to say.

'It's about them socials and that,' replied Dean. 'You know, like the Chess Club thing.'

Wesley smiled, just a little. 'Oh yes,' he said.

'Well, it's like this,' began Dean, 'I wanna know if they ever take like a register at them things . . . you know, does anyone ever check who's there and who's not?'

Wesley considered what Dean had said like it was some maths problem that he'd been set. He looked at me, smiled just a little more and then cleared his throat as if he was about to say something really important.

'Well, Mr Wilson comes in now and then but he doesn't—'

'And are you in any other clubs?' interrupted Dean.

Wesley went back to beetroot.

'Er . . . I . . . er . . .' he stammered.

I decided that it was time for a little feminine charm.

'Hi – *Wes* – can I call you Wes?'

'Um . . . er . . .' he replied. I was just waiting for him to say mummy.

'So, Wes, *do you* go to any other socials?' I continued, smiling at him.

He coughed and looked down at his feet.

'Yes . . . I . . . er . . . attend Science Club on Thursdays,' he told us.

'Oh,' I whispered, moving closer to him and putting my hand on his arm. 'And what about any others?'

He looked at my hand like it was a monster's claw.

'We're . . . we're not allowed to . . .'

I moved my face even closer to his, knowing that Dean was smirking.

'I know that, Wes, but you seem kind of clever to me.

I'm *sure* someone like you knows *all kinds* of ways to avoid the rules. Come on . . . just between *us*,' I whispered.

Wesley started to edge backwards, away from my face, but he came to the wall and had to stop. I moved further towards him, trapping him against the wall. He looked up at my eyes and gulped. I was dying to laugh but held it back.

'Well?' I said, almost into his ear.

'Yes . . . *yes*!' he shouted. 'I do attend more than I should . . . *I do . . . I do!*'

Dean started laughing and I had to bite my lip to stop myself from joining in. Wesley stepped away and told me the rest.

'I attend four a week,' he said. 'I know it's wrong but you won't tell anyone will you?'

'No, no, Wes – this will be our little secret,' I replied.

'It's just that no one checks and it's all a bit of harmless fun,' he continued, smiling a little.

'Yeah – OK, Wesley,' I said, 'I get the picture.'

Only Wesley didn't catch my drift and carried on talking. 'And Robert and I, we thought, well what the—'

'Wesley,' said Dean.

'Er . . . yes?' he replied.

'Shut up . . . there's a good little boy.'

'Er . . . OK, Dean. See you both in Chess Club?' he half-stated, half-asked.

'I can hardly wait,' I told him, in a breathless voice.

Wesley scampered off up the stairs and Dean poked me in the arm.

'Man, you are harsh . . . playing up to him like that.'

'I don't know *what* you mean,' I replied, smiling slyly.

'He thinks he's in there . . .' laughed Dean.

'Er *yeah* . . . like in his wildest *dreams*.'

Later that morning, Dean and I left Mr Herbert's lesson early and the looks we got from Hannah, Imtiaz and Suky told me that we were going to have to tell them about our scam very soon. All afternoon, they just talked amongst themselves, hardly allowing Dean or myself to join in with their conversations. When I complained though, Dean laughed at me.

'Jealous. Don't worry about it.'

'But I *am* worried about it. They're our friends.'

'It's no big deal, Sister Gee.'

TROUBLE

'We're going to have to tell them,' I said, more to myself. Dean had stopped listening and was busy telling me that we had to pick some more socials.

'. . . Fridays we get to miss some of CDT . . . Tuesdays we'll miss ten minutes of Geography . . . this is wicked! *And* no more concrete chips ever again!'

I looked at him and shook my head.

TEN

There was no sign of Jit the next morning either. I had toast crumbs on my jumper and Dean was telling me to brush them off as we walked up to the school, late again. Mr Black was waiting at the gate, holding a clipboard.

'Good morning,' he said in a loud jolly voice as we meandered in.

'Morning, sir,' both of us said in unison.

'Yes – and a fine morning too – sunny and bright with just a touch of autumn chill. Just the kind of morning on which I'd expect my pupils to be up bright and early. *Bright and early* . . .' he said, looking at us inquisitively.

'Sorry, sir.'

'*Sorry . . .?* You're not *sorry*. If you were anywhere approaching *sorry* you would attempt to get to school on time for a change,' he told us, without changing his tone.

I exchanged a look with Dean as Mr Black smiled away, like a demented puppet.

'You're going to have to learn that behind the motto lies an iron will,' he told us, still smiling.

'Yes, sir,' I said, wondering what he was on about. I didn't have to wait long to find out.

'Detention . . . from Monday evening, Miss Parkhurst. That goes for you too, Mr Chambers, and the rest of this sorry band.'

He gestured with an arm towards the other pupils sauntering slowly up the road.

'*RIGHT!* Get in line the lot of you!' he shouted breezily as everyone moaned and complained.

'Name and form group on this clipboard, please,' he told them all. 'In life you'll find that not many people are given the number of second chances that I allow my pupils. But then you know me – firm but fair. *Firm but fair.*'

I wrote my name and form number down on the clipboard before handing it to Dean, who looked at it like I'd handed him a mouldy fish or something. He wrote down his details and we made our way to the door.

'Monday night, you two . . . assembly hall. One hour

– you can let your parents know over the weekend. And the rest of you – don't bother to write down the names of imaginary pupils. I know who all of you are,' said Black, *still* smiling.

'What a lovely morning,' he said again, as Dean and I headed for our form room.

We arrived to find Mrs Dooher in a bad mood. Well, bad for her, anyway. She wasn't smiling at all and she had already taken the register when we joined the gang.

'I've got a note here from Mr Black,' she said, standing up, 'about late attendances.' She looked at Dean and myself. 'And I believe that you two are the prime offenders.'

'But miss—' Dean began only to be cut off.

'But nothing, Dean . . . there's always an excuse.'

'The bus don't come until whenever and then there's always traffic and that,' he continued, unfazed.

'Yes – the infamous "late bus",' said Mrs Dooher with more than a touch of sarcasm. 'The only problem with that theory is that our wonderful principal has undertaken to *time* when it arrives at the stop. And he *also* timed how long it takes to walk from said bus stop to the school gate.'

'Man's a weirdo,' laughed Imi.

'He may well be, but he does have a point,' said Mrs Dooher. 'That particular bus, the 42, gets to the stop fifteen minutes before you are due at school. It's no more than a five minute walk from the stop to the school gates so somewhere there's a missing ten minutes.'

Someone shouted out '*DUN DUN DERRR!*' at the idea of the mysterious missing minutes and Mrs Dooher broke into a grin.

'Whatever the ins and outs,' she continued, 'the upshot is that anyone who is late from now on will be subject to detention in the assembly hall on Monday evenings.'

'Huh?' asked Suky, looking at Hannah.

'Yeah – like what if you're late on a Wednesday?' added Imi.

'Then you will have to put your name on the clip-board at the gate and attend mass detention the following Monday.'

'That's just mad, that is,' said Suky.

'Mass detention . . . what we gonna get next, miss – army induction training before chemistry?' Hannah asked.

'And what about people who are late every day?' asked a boy called Dilip from the back.

Everyone looked at me and Dean. I went red and looked down at the desk. Dean just shrugged and grinned.

'Yeah,' added Imi, 'how is that fair? If I'm late one day and someone *else* is late every day, then I get the same punishment as *that* person,' he finished, pointing at Dean.

'Calm down, class . . . the whole point of the exercise is to weed out the *persistent* offenders,' Mrs Dooher told us, reading straight from Mr Black's notes.

'Yeah but it ain't fair is it?' continued Imi. 'Just because some of us are mature enough to get to school on time and some aren't – why should we all suffer?'

'But if you're not late then why would it bother you, Mr Dhondy?' pointed out Mrs Dooher. Imi shrugged, conceding the point.

'Still not fair,' said Suky, backing up Imi, like she always did.

Mrs Dooher was about to say something more but the bell went and everyone groaned and stood up, grabbing their stuff.

'School's *nuts*, man,' said one pupil.

'*Principal*'s nuts,' said another. 'That's what my dad reckons . . . imagine calling it Devana High and then getting that nutter to run it.'

'*My* dad,' said a third pupil, a girl called Heather, 'reckons that Mr Black used to take loads of drugs in the Sixties and that.'

'*Whass the Sixties?*' asked Dilip, looking confused, as Mrs Dooher ushered us off to our lessons.

At break Hannah and I were sitting on the steps that led up to the tennis courts, watching the older boys playing football. There was one in particular, a lad in Year Ten called Billy, who we both thought was fit. Hannah was watching him as he played, but my mind was on Jit and what was wrong with him. I was trying to get Hannah to pay attention and it was hard going.

'Are you listening to me?' I asked for the fifth time.

'Yeah – course I'm listening. I can do more than two things at the same time, you know.'

'Yes – but are you paying attention?'

'Not quite in the way that you'd like me to, no,' she said with a grin.

'Hannah!'

'What . . . ? Oh . . . Jit. Look, I went round to see him last night.'

'*And?*' God, she was winding me up.

'And what? He opened the door and stood there like a weirdo. Didn't even invite me in.'

'Did he look sick?' I asked.

'Depends on what you mean by sick I suppose,' she replied, not looking at me.

'What's that supposed to mean? How many ways are there to look sick?'

'Hmmm?' she mumbled, twisting round so that she could watch Billy from a better angle.

'Hannah!'

Hannah finally turned to look at me.

'What? Er . . . he looked normal. There wasn't like a big sign on his forehead saying "living dead" or anything. He just stood there and asked me what I wanted.'

'And . . . ?'

'You fancy him or something?'

'No!' I protested.

'Just, the way you've been with Dean lately anyone would think that you and *him* had something going on,' she added, turning her full attention to me now that Billy had walked off.

'What you on about?'

'Well! All that going around in secret and leaving lessons and stuff – what's that all about?' she asked.

'Nothing – you'll find out soon enough. You could say we're doing some research for everyone else. Kind of testing the water,' I winked at her. Well, I tried anyway.

'Yeah – what*ever* . . . anyway, Jit was his usual strange self. You know – rude, mardy . . .'

'Did you ask him if he was ill, Hannah?'

'Yeah – he said he had a cough and then he told me that he wanted to go to bed and shut the door in my face.'

I gave her a surprised look. She saw it and shrugged.

'Don't worry – he's fine. I've told you so many times, Grace – he's a nutter. *Lovely* but nuts – ever since he was a kid. He gets really odd sometimes . . .'

Something in my nosy investigator head perked up and took notice. 'Why do you think he's like that then?' I asked.

Hannah shrugged and looked away for a moment. She said something about him having had a rough time as a kid. I was sure she knew more but I let it go. She was Jit's oldest and closest friend, with Dean. She was bound to know more about him than anyone else. I just wanted to know too.

'That Billy is lovely,' said Hannah, changing the subject. She got up and wiped her clothes down.

'He's all right,' I said, standing up too, ready to go back to lessons.

'Yeah – you wouldn't mind if he asked you out.'

I smiled as we headed indoors. 'I'd tell him that my diary was full,' I insisted.

'I bet,' Hannah said, and laughed.

In the next lesson, History, Dean passed me a note. I waited for Mr Woods to turn to the board before I opened it.

On Fridays it's Computer Club! Let's join up! What do you think?

I looked at Dean and smiled. Imi saw me and asked what was in the note.

'Nothing,' I whispered back.

'Yeah – looks like it,' he replied, just a little too loudly.

'Imtiaz . . . something to share?' asked Mr Woods.

'Er . . . no, sir,' he replied, looking down at his pad and doodling.

I nodded at Dean and tried to wink again.

ELEVEN

I spent most of Saturday morning trying to call at Jit's house. My dad was busy and my mum was away. Hannah came round at lunch time to do some homework. She'd called for Jit on the way to mine. No one had answered again. By the time that we'd finished our work it was mid-afternoon. I decided that I would ride back to Hannah's on my bike so that I could call for Jit, something that I'd only done three times before. Hannah told me that I was mad.

'There's nothing up with him – nothing *physical* anyway,' she told me, as we walked back to hers.

'I just want to see if he's all right,' I protested, wondering why she thought it was such a big deal.

'That's probably what he wants you to do – it's just an act with him,' replied Hannah.

'Why would he put on an act?' I asked.

'Come on, Grace. It's obvious he likes you, but he

has to be the centre of attention all the time. He's still a baby really.'

'He *doesn't like me*,' I said, not really believing my own words.

'Yes he does and you've been spending loads of time with Dean. I reckon he's just a little bit jealous,' she told me, smiling and shaking her head at the confused look on my face. Mainly because she knew that I was putting it on.

'It was only a bit of fun – we were going to tell you all about it.'

'Yeah . . . whatever,' smiled Hannah. 'Knowing Dean it's gonna be some crack-head scheme.'

'Don't you mean crack pot?' I asked, frowning.

'No, Grace – I mean crack-*head*.'

We both giggled.

'Seriously though, he doesn't *fancy* me . . . not Jit.'

'Grace – you *know* that he does and I think that you like him too.' This time Hannah grinned alone.

'Don't,' I protested.

'Do,' she answered.

'Don't!'

'DO! Do-do-do-do-do!'

I gave Hannah a funny look. An Asian couple

walking past gave her the same look. As did an old white woman walking her dog. Even the *dog* gave her . . . well *OK* . . . maybe not the dog.

'God, that was like being back at primary school, wasn't it?' she asked me, embarrassed.

'Yes,' I told her. 'Infants even.'

We walked past a huge mosque and an infant school. Hannah's house was still five minutes walk away and Jit's another five minutes after that. I realized again just how far Jit walked in the mornings to catch the same bus as me.

'He's quite fit,' I said completely out of the blue, as we arrived at Hannah's street.

'Who?' she asked me, looking around to see who I was on about.

'Jit . . . well, he will be fit – when he's matured a bit.'

Hannah grinned again. '*See*? Told you.'

'I don't fancy him *now*,' I said, 'but I can see that I might – you know – when we're like in Year Ten or something?'

'He *is* good looking,' agreed Hannah before screwing up her face. 'I couldn't go *out* with him though – he's like my brother.'

'Not now . . . but I can see why girls might fancy

him . . .' I continued, not really knowing where I was going with my point.

'And you're as weird as he is. What do you mean you can see how he might be fit – you fancy him. You *already* think he's fit,' laughed Hannah

'Yeah – but I wouldn't go out with him – I don't want a boyfriend yet . . . it's just too . . .'

'*Normal?*' asked Hannah, having a joke at my expense.

'Get lost,' I replied.

'I am,' she told me. 'See you Monday.'

She walked down the street to her house as I set off for Jit's. When I arrived at his mum's house the curtains were drawn and I could hear music coming from inside. Reggae. I pressed the bell and waited. After a few moments I pressed it again. Across the street a group of lads wolf whistled and asked me if I was checkin' anyone. I ignored them and rang the bell again, following up the ring with a knock on the door. The music went off and I heard someone moving about. I waited impatiently as the door opened and Jit stuck his head out, blinking at the daylight that flooded in. He looked surprised to see me.

'Er . . . hi, Grace,' he said sheepishly, as I stood there.

'Hi!' I replied cheerfully. 'Just thought I'd come round and see what was up with you.'

'Yeah . . . er . . . I'm fine. Just had a bit of a cold, that's all,' he told me.

'Oh. You don't look like you've got a . . .' I began, before thinking better of it and changing the subject. 'So, can I come in or something?'

Jit looked confused for a moment before he spoke. 'Er . . . look, why don't we go back round to yours,' he replied quickly.

I looked at him like he was mad.

'It's just that my mum's asleep and . . .'

'But you just had your music on dead loud,' I pointed out.

'Er . . . look, can we please just go round to yours – the house is a mess and—'

'Yeah, yeah. OK,' I said, relenting. 'I suppose we can head back to mine – but you're a very strange boy.'

I smiled at him. Jit looked away and mumbled something about grabbing his jacket. He closed the door on me and went off, returning a few moments later wearing a jacket and with slightly dampened hair.

I think that he'd sprayed some deodorant too judging by the smell coming from him.

'Are you OK?' I asked.

'Yeah!' he replied, as we walked back down the street.

'Weirdo . . . anyone would think you had something hidden at your house the way you go on.'

'It's nothing – I told you. The house is a mess and I was feeling a bit embarrassed and—'

'Yeah, whatever. You don't need to explain to me,' I interrupted, sweetly.

I did want to know why he wouldn't let me in but at the same time I didn't want to embarrass him. We walked down the main road, past Hannah's street, and back towards the mosque. There we took the left-hand fork in the road, crossed over and walked down to Holmfield Road which led back towards where I lived. I saw a group of lads heading away from us. One of them was Jason Patel. I looked at Jit.

'It's Jason,' I said.

Jit nodded. 'We'd better go the long way round,' he said, and we didn't speak until we got to my house.

Inside, my dad emerged from the front room, which was his study.

'Ah, Jit! Just the man. I wonder, could you help me with a little problem?'

'Er . . . yeah – go on then,' replied Jit, smiling for the first time since I'd knocked on his door.

'Great! Come in to the office,' said my dad, as we both followed him in.

His office was its usual messy self with books and papers lying on every surface, including the wooden floor. He cleared a space around his rickety desk, which looked like it might fall apart at any minute. The walls were bare except for a couple of posters and a photo of my dad with some old guitarist called Mick Jones, who he idolized. I didn't even know who he was. One of dad's building designs was lying on the desk top and Jit moved closer to take a look at it.

'I'm working on that right now,' Dad said, 'but that's not what I wanted your help with.'

'Dad?'

'Relax, Grace – it's just something that I wanted to run by Jit. And you too . . .' he added quickly.

'What is it, Mr Parkhurst?' asked Jit, curious.

'I'm considering replacing my stereo system, Jit. The one I've got is something that I bought before Grace was born and I've been reading up about these new systems . . . you know – all singing, all dancing type affairs.'

He beamed at Jit. Jit looked at me with amusement. I groaned and shrugged.

'Dad!'

'Come on, Grace – it'll be fun,' replied my dad, pulling a pile of magazines from under his desk.

'I've got *What Hi-Fi, Hi-Fi Weekly*, a couple of dealer catalogues and some reviews from the internet,' he said proudly.

My dad was a firm believer in good research. When our last telly had blown up he'd borrowed a black-and-white portable from my uncle and then spent three months trying to decide which new telly to buy. Three months of watching everything in gloomy, dull, black and white. Eventually he'd settled for this huge plasma TV with internet and 3D and all this other stuff that excited Jit and Dean. Boy's toys.

'Cool,' said Jit.

I sighed. It looked like I was going to have to wait to find out what was up with him.

'You'll stay for dinner obviously, Jit?' beamed my dad.

'Er . . . If that's all right,' replied Jit, unsure of himself and looking to me for confirmation.

'You always do anyway,' I said, shaking my head and smiling.

'Lovely – I think we'll get a takeaway – just remember to let your mum know,' my dad told him, opening the first magazine. 'Now what do you think to this ensemble . . .'

In the end Jit and my dad spent three hours trying to work out which system would be best, while I went off and watched TV, which was boring. The only things on were game shows and competitions where talentless idiots attempted to convince old people with long hair and sunglasses that they should allow them to make pop music. I ended up watching a documentary on the contribution of immigrants to Britain's culture and economy, taking notes to impress my teachers with. There was a whole section on Leicester too, so as I watched I tried to see if I could recognize streets and shops and stuff. Jit and my dad came in around eight o'clock and plumped themselves down on a sofa.

'Right, Jit – what shall we have for dinner?' said my dad.

'You might as well adopt him and be done,' I

replied, a little annoyed that I hadn't been asked what I wanted for dinner.

'Come on now, Grace, there's no need for that – Jit's a guest in our house, not to mention one of your best friends,' said my dad.

'Yeah – sorry,' I offered. 'It's just that he came round to see *me* and you borrowed him all night for your silly research thing.'

My dad came over, ruffled my hair and then gave me a kiss, before saying 'Poor Gracey' in a silly voice.

'GERROFF!' I giggled as he tickled me.

In the end I fell off the sofa and lay on the floor, red faced and with tears in my eyes. I looked up at Jit who was smiling and stuck my tongue out at him. My dad left the room and came back a few moments later with takeaway menus – Chinese, Indian and Italian. We opted for Chinese and ordered it. The takeaway was around the corner from the house so Jit and I waited ten minutes and then walked round to pick it up. I asked him what was up with him as we sat in the takeaway, getting hungrier and hungrier as the smell of food emerged from the kitchen at the back.

'It's just that you and Dean have been ignoring me,' he replied after a while, not looking at me.

'We haven't been *ignoring* you – we've just been . . . *researching* something,' I told him.

'What?' he asked, picking up the edge of a magazine with his finger and thumb.

'Nothing . . . it's still a secret,' I said.

'*See?* You two are keeping secrets from me,' he protested.

'Jit – honestly it's nothing.'

'I don't believe you,' he said in a sullen tone.

'*God!* You're like a kid sometimes,' I snapped.

The woman behind the counter looked at us for a moment and then smiled and continued to read her magazine. Jit sat for a while and then he looked at me.

'So tell me what it is if it's not such a big thing,' he said.

'Oh all right then . . . it's those socials that Dean was on about – you know, all that stuff about missing late lunches and eating cold food and . . .'

I explained it all to him as we waited for the food order, and then on the short walk home we came up with a little trick that we could play on Dean. That seemed to cheer Jit up, and by the time my dad gave him a lift home at ten o'clock he seemed to be in a really good mood and told me that he'd see me on Monday morning. I thought back to what Hannah had said about Jit wanting to be at the centre of things all the time and decided that she had been right. But she was wrong about him fancying me . . . stinky pants girl.

TWELVE

The following Wednesday morning we were all sitting in Maths with Mrs Lee-Cross, working on problems that she'd set. Jit held up his hand halfway through the lesson and when Mrs Lee-Cross asked what he wanted, he told her that he needed to talk to her in private. She gave him a concerned look and then asked him to go with her out into the corridor. Jit got up and followed her, not looking at any of us. As soon as the door closed behind them the entire class started to chat amongst themselves, beginning quietly and then raising their voices when they didn't hear the usual 'Shut up' command from the teacher. Dean was the first one of our group to make a comment about Jit.

'He's skivin' again,' he said to no one in particular.

'His business. He's the one gonna be stuck at the end of the year asking us to help him with his work,' replied Imtiaz.

'Well he wasn't well last week,' I chipped in, defending him.

'Yeah right – he's *desperately* ill,' laughed Suky.

'He's a weirdo – I keep telling you,' added Hannah.

I looked away, trying not to grin. Mrs Lee-Cross came back a few minutes later and asked the class to quieten down. She had this look on her face that was a cross between embarrassment and concern and I wondered what Jit had said to her.

We spent the rest of the lesson going over the problems that we had been set and ten minutes before the end Mrs Lee-Cross nodded at Wesley and Robert. They stood up and Dean and I used that as our cue to leave too. Hannah sighed as we left and called us part-timers.

'That'll be enough, Miss Meadows, said Mrs Lee-Cross. 'Perhaps you could talk us through the next problem . . .'

I followed Dean to the dinner hall where we both grabbed some food and I watched as Dean threw his chips and beans down his throat. He might as well have tipped the whole plate down there, he ate them so fast. I kept my sandwiches for the Chess Club and we were outside the room before the bell had even gone for lunch. I stopped at the door, looked in, and then turned to Dean.

'Ooh, we've got a new boy,' I said, smiling.

'Nice one! Another lamb to the slaughter,' laughed Dean. 'Which nerd we got this week then?'

He opened the door and I waited for him to enter but he just stood where he was, his mouth wide open like a tunnel.

'How the . . . ?' he began as I broke into laughter.

'Yes, Dean!' shouted Jit. 'I thought I'd come check out the nerd zone, innit.'

Dean turned to me and started to say something else only I interrupted him.

'I had to tell him, Dean. He forced it out of me . . . honest!' I lied, smiling as widely as I could.

'So what do you do with these things then?' asked Jit, picking up a knight.

Wesley, who was in there already, smiled at me and started to explain the role of the knight and its position on the board, only for Jit to hold up his hand and cut him off.

'I'm asking my devious friend over there – not you,' he told Wesley, whose face went bright red.

'Who yuh call devious?' asked Dean, aggressively.

'You!' replied Jit in the same tone.

Both of them squared up to each other and the rest of the group froze, thinking that there was going to be a fight. I thought so too until I saw the smiles break on both their faces.

'You is one sly man, bro,' laughed Jit, throwing the chess piece at Dean, who ducked as it whistled past him.

From behind us came a plopping sound and an 'Oh'. We turned to see Mr Wilson standing in the doorway, with splashes of coffee on his glasses. Jit had somehow managed to get the piece to land in Wilson's coffee mug.

'All right, sir,' smiled Dean as Mr Wilson wiped off his glasses on his lab coat.

'Er . . . yes, I'm absolutely fine,' replied Wilson. 'Er . . . I'm afraid that I can't recall your . . .' He looked at Dean quizzically.

'It's Dean, sir. Dean . . . Patel.'

'Well, Mr Patel, it's time you got down to some chess, isn't it?'

Jit and me grinned at Dean's joke and then started to put the pieces on the boards. Well, I put them on the board. Jit was trying to get them to do rude things to each other.

'Jit!' I said, shaking my head. 'That's so childish.'

'Yeah, Jit,' smiled Dean, joining us, 'when you gonna grow up?'

'I never knew Imi had a twin brother,' replied Jit, removing the queen's head from the king's backside.

'We gonna tell *them* too, I suppose?' said Dean, looking at me.

'We should – they're our friends. It'll be fun, all of us in Chess Club and Book Club and God knows what else.'

Jit gave Dean another of his looks.

'What – you mean you're in more than one?' he asked.

'Yeah,' replied Dean. 'Didn't the world's worst secret agent, *Double-OH-Nuttin*, tell you?'

'When's that?'

'Thursdays and then on Fridays it's Computers and that.'

Jit smiled. 'Wicked! No more late lunches . . . let's sign up for everything, bro,' he said excitedly.

'We'll have to be careful that we don't get caught,' I said, cautiously.

'Why?' asked Dean. 'We're on detention every Monday for the rest of the year *anyways* – what else can they do?'

I thought about it and realized that he was probably right. We'd been late every morning that week and were due at the mass detention the following Monday anyway. And no doubt there would be more too. Then a sly grin spread across my face.

'We don't ever have the same teacher before lunch twice do we?' I said.

Jit and Dean thought about it for a moment and then agreed.

'Right,' I continued, 'and no one takes a register or anything?'

'Yeah,' they both said.

'So what's to stop us joining a club for *every* lunch time?'

They looked at each other and then both of them grinned at the same time.

'*See?* They say it's the kids like us that cause all the fuss but when you check it – it's the nice, cute posh girls that get *us* into trouble,' laughed Dean.

'What if we do get caught?' added Jit.

I smiled. 'No problem – I'll just tell my dad that you led me astray.'

For a moment Jit thought that I was being serious.

'You can't do that, man . . . he'll batter me,' he replied.

'Like I would tell him,' I said. 'And anyway – he'd just laugh and say that you were a lad, Jit. He's softer on you than he is on me . . . and he lets you pick what we're going to eat.'

'What?' asked Dean, confused.

'Private joke,' I said, trying to wink at Jit and failing.

Dean did the exact opposite to what Jit would have done if I'd have said that to him. He told me to take my private joke and stuff it. Jit would have just gone funny for the rest of the day. Someone told us to keep the noise down, but when we turned to see who it was, everyone was staring at their own games.

'Nerds, man,' laughed Jit, smiling at me like I had just given him a million pounds or something.

THIRTEEN

We missed ten minutes of English with Mr Herbert the following day and ten minutes of Design and Technology on the Friday morning. By the time we were all leaving to go home, Hannah, Suky and Imi were really unhappy with us. At the bus stop they stood together and when Dean tried to get Imi to listen to his 'Herbert Rap', Imi moved away and told him that he wasn't interested. Not that it stopped Dean, who rapped it anyway, entertaining the rest of the pupils. They liked it so much that some of them got Dean to repeat the lyrics over and over so that they could learn it too. Eventually there were about twenty kids rapping along, as the bus made its way through the traffic. Not that the other three heard it. They sat on the lower deck to avoid us and I seemed to be the only one bothered by it.

'We have to tell them,' I told Jit. 'They're not stupid – they'll work it out soon enough.'

'How? The socials are like a secret society. I bet Wesley and them have special handshakes and that,' replied Jit, unfazed.

'It's not a joke, Jit. I'm telling them.'

'When?' said Jit, smiling at Dean.

'*Now!*' I replied, getting up as the bus rounded a corner. Not the cleverest thing to do.

I stumbled down the stairs onto the lower deck, ignored the laughter from the back and sat down on Hannah's knee.

'*Gerroff you nutcase!*' she screamed as I kissed her on the cheek.

'Come round later,' I said, smiling. 'There's something that I want to tell you.' I looked at the seat behind where Suky and Imi were pretending that I didn't exist.

'I want both of you to come too!' I beamed.

They looked at each other and ignored me.

'*Please . . . !*' I begged. 'Please, please, please!'

'Why?' asked Suky.

'I want to tell you what me and Dean have been up to,' I replied.

'What makes you think that we care?' asked Imtiaz, screwing up his face.

'Because if you *didn't* care then you wouldn't be so angry about it, ignoring us and sitting downstairs.'

'Maybe we just want to act our ages for a change?' said Imtiaz.

'Oh get a sense of humour, idiot boy!' I told him, grinning. 'Come round at six . . . I'll get dad to make dinner for us all.'

'Yeah all right,' replied Hannah, 'but gerroff me will you – my leg's going to sleep.'

'Okey cokey,' I said in a silly voice. 'See you all later.'

Hannah grinned, Suky smiled and Imi shrugged his shoulders. I knew they'd turn up though. They always did.

We had vegetable lasagne for dinner and my dad was really off on one, telling the gang all about his new stereo, which he could link up to his laptop to download MP3 files from the internet, and which included loads of other gadgets which might as well have been from another planet as far as I was concerned. I eventually got him to stop talking about it around seven o'clock. We went down to the cellar as my dad started to collect the dishes, a sullen look on his face, like I'd spoiled his party or something. My mum just laughed and called him a child, as she went off to the living room to relax after work.

Down in the cellar, Dean and Jit racked up the pool balls and started to play as Imtiaz and the girls sat on the sofa and waited for me to tell them what had been going on.

'OK, smelly bums – the reason I asked you to come round was to tell you about what Dean and I have been up to,' I told them, smiling.

Imtiaz pretended to yawn and Suky looked at her hands. Hannah was watching Dean and Jit play pool. Not the reaction that I was hoping for.

'*Well* . . . ?' I said.

'Well *what*?' replied Imi.

'Ask me about it then,' I urged, convinced that they *did* care.

'All right – how is *it*?' asked Suky with a sad attempt at humour.

'Doh! Nice try,' replied Jit, waiting for Dean to take his shot.

'Get stuffed, Bhangra Boy,' she replied in turn, forcing a smile out of Hannah.

'Oh get on with it,' Imi said, sounding bored.

'We've been researchin' stuff,' Dean told them, missing his shot by a couple of inches.

'Yeah – researchin' yer ass,' said Hannah.

'Is that how you got it, *yeah*?' Dean asked her, grinning.

'Oh for God's sake – what are you on about?' said Suky, raising her voice.

'*Well*, you know how Dean was complaining about having to go to late lunches? We've found a way to get out of them. Forever.'

'Is this the important thing you had to tell us?' asked Imtiaz. 'That's so lame . . . who cares?'

'So you're quite happy to eat cold chips and warm sandwiches and that?' Jit replied.

'Well no, but it ain't going to ruin my life or nothing,' said Imtiaz.

'Depends on what you eat,' added Dean. 'I seen this thing on the telly 'bout food poisoning and that . . . food can kill you, you know.'

'Shut up, Dean,' said Suky.

'Easy, sister!' laughed Dean.

'Oh shut up, all of you!' I shouted. 'I'm trying to tell you something.'

Everyone looked at me in surprise. I ignored them and carried on.

'We found out about these lunch time socials that the school runs. Clubs that you can go to from Tuesday to Friday. Dean joined one and then so did I and they're cool.'

'Socials?' asked Hannah, raising her eyebrows.

'Yeah, like the Book Club and Computers,' I replied.

'*And* Chess,' grinned Jit. 'Don't forget to tell them about Chess.'

'*Chess?*' said Imtiaz, looking disgusted.

I looked at him and then at the girls.

'Er . . . yeah . . . Chess too . . . anyway. The thing is – if you join one of these clubs then you get to leave lessons ten minutes early so that you can get your dinner and then get to the club.'

'Hot food, my friends – every day . . . *believe!*' added Dean, like he was talking about treasure.

'And the teacher can't say anything about it because they're like part of the social life of the school . . . only no one knows about them. No one cool anyway . . .'

'Yeah,' agreed Jit, 'they're like geek heaven. Wesley and Robert go to them but they're open to everyone.'

'And that's where you've been disappearing off to?' asked Suky.

'Yes,' I told her.

'And you can go to one every day?' she continued.

'Well not on Mondays because they don't run then. And actually, strictly speaking, you can only join two,' I replied, looking to Jit and Dean for support.

'Yeah but no one don't check or anything,' added Dean.

'*Doesn't* check, Chambers,' scolded Hannah, mocking him, but getting it wrong herself, too.

'Ehh! Check out *Likkle Miss Dictionary* . . . chill, man. Don't get all discombobulated or nothin'.'

Everyone stopped what they were doing and looked at Dean.

'*Dis-com-what-a-lated?*' asked Imi, amazed.

'And you reckon *I've* swallowed a dictionary,' grinned Hannah.

'What's it mean anyway?' said Jit.

'Bet he don't even know!' teased Suky.

'Course I do, man. I man is the lyrics officer . . . words is my business!' replied Dean.

'So tell us what it means,' insisted Imtiaz.

'It means upset, man. Or uncomfortable,' Dean told him proudly.

'Man, you really *are* spending too much time with Wesley Magoogan,' said Hannah, grinning again.

'Getting back to the socials – are you saying that we can join one every day?' asked Suky.

'Yes,' I replied. 'There's no register taken and the teachers just turn up and say hello before running off to do whatever.'

'It's a blag . . . no worries,' added Jit.

'But surely someone will work it out?' asked Imtiaz, suddenly interested.

I smiled.

'See – I knew it would get your attention,' I told him. 'So far we've joined three – but this week coming we're going to join one more.'

'You're mad,' said Hannah. 'You'll get caught.'

'So what?' replied Dean. 'We're in detention every Monday anyway . . . what else can they do?'

'And you never have to go for late lunch again?' asked Suky.

'No late lunch, no getting wet in the rain, no freezing to death, huddled up against a wall in winter . . . heaven,' I told her.

'And the clubs ain't that bad either,' said Jit, supporting me. 'It'll be a right laugh if we all join the same ones.'

'I dunno,' Imtiaz said. 'It's OK to talk about it, but what if we get caught?'

'We ain't just talking are we?' Dean reminded him. 'We've researched it . . . and Wesley and the nerds get away with it so why shouldn't we?'

'You mean they go to more than they should?' asked Hannah, amazed.

'Yes – we were shocked too,' I replied. 'Wesley breaking the rules . . . kind of strange but true. I asked him myself.'

'I bet he nearly wet his pants,' Imi said, laughing.

'Urgh! You stinky boy!' I said, screwing up my face. That wasn't an image I wanted in my head – thank you *very* much.

'So you lot gonna join or what?' asked Dean.

'Hush up and take your shot,' Jit told him.

'Stand back then, little boy. Watch how a big man play the game.'

I grinned at the gang.

'I'm going upstairs to ask your mum for a dictionary,' said Hannah.

'Why?' I asked.

'To check out Dean's big word . . . bet he's lying,' she told me.

'*Check it, check it, 'cos you know you can't test it!*' rapped Dean, missing his shot by a mile.

FOURTEEN

Imtiaz, Suky and Hannah joined Chess Club first, coming along the following Wednesday. The look on Mrs Lee-Cross' face when we all got up to leave Maths was a picture, but she didn't try to stop us. Instead, she said that she was pleased that young people were willing to take up such an ancient and exciting game. I barely kept my snigger under my breath as we walked out and headed for the dining hall. The club was in full flow when we got there and no one said anything about us being there, not even Willy Wilson, who congratulated Dean on bringing him 'fresh troops', as he called the gang.

'Well done, Mr Patel,' he said, walking out of the room just as Hannah and Suky were about to tell him that Dean's surname was actually Chambers.

'What's that all about?' they asked me as Dean tried to play a game against Wesley and Robert.

'Just a little joke,' I replied. 'So – what do you think then?'

'It's all right . . . can't play chess though,' answered Suky.

'That's the whole point of the club – to learn the game,' I told her.

'Nah,' said Hannah, 'the whole point is to get out of late lunches . . . I don't want to learn how to play this stupid game.'

I smirked at her.

'It's not stupid though, is it? It's an ancient and venerable game of strategy and intellect.'

'Yeah, like, what-*ever*!' replied Suky in a fake American accent. Holding her hand out in my face.

Hannah picked up a queen.

'What's this one do?' she asked.

'That's the queen . . . she's the strongest piece on the board,' came a reply from behind us.

We turned to find Wesley looking at us, pushing his glasses back up his nose. He was bright red but trying to hide his embarrassment with a smile.

'And who exactly asked you, Wesley?' said Suky.

Wesley shifted uncomfortably.

'Don't be so rude, Suky,' said Hannah, smiling

at the poor lad as I tried not to laugh.

'*Poor Wesley* . . . why don't you tell us *all* about it?' she said to him.

'Well . . . um . . . er . . . it's the best piece. It can do anything.'

Hannah leaned towards him with her head cocked to one side, mischief in her eyes.

'*Anything?*' she whispered.

'Er . . . um . . .' replied Wesley, not sure where to look.

'Now, that's a game I *like*,' she continued, 'a game where the *strongest* piece is a woman.'

'I . . . er . . . I m-must get b-back . . . er . . .' stammered Wesley, turning around and fleeing back to his friends.

Suky and I nearly fell off our chairs we were laughing so much. I had tears streaming down my face. The lads had watched it all and were shaking their heads.

'Man, you girls are evil!' laughed Jit, holding his sides.

'Pure wickedness, bro,' agreed Dean.

'Funny though,' Imtiaz pointed out.

Later that afternoon I was walking to my final lesson

with Dean and Jit, when Jit stopped to go to the loo. As Dean and I waited outside in the corridor he told me about some girl he liked in the year above us, Monica.

'She asked me out,' Dean said, as a gang of older lads pushed past us. 'Watch it!' he shouted.

One of the lads, Marcus Thomas, turned round and glared at Dean. 'You what? You gotta problem?'

Dean gulped and apologized, looking away.

'Didn't think so, likkle bwoi!' replied Marcus, before joining his friends.

'You really know how to get into trouble, don't you,' I said.

'Man, I thought he was going to kick my head in!' Dean replied, with relief in his voice.

Just then Jit walked out of the boys' loo.

'You best go in there, Dean,' he said, all seriously.

'Why, what you sayin' – that I've *pooped* my pants?' answered Dean.

'You *what?*' replied Jit, confused. He hadn't seen the argument with Marcus. I grinned.

'Just go in the toilets, bro. There's something written on the wall that you better see.'

'What?' I asked, getting all nosy.

'Yeah what, Jit?' repeated Dean.

'Just go check it out,' urged Jit.

Dean walked through the door and was gone for a minute or so. When he came back out into the corridor he was grinning.

'Yes! The road to fame and fortune begins right here,' he exclaimed.

'What are you two banging on about?' I asked, wondering what was written on the wall.

'Someone's written the words to the "Herbert Rap" on the wall,' said Dean with pride.

'Yeah and that means he's gonna find out about it and then you're in big trouble,' Jit pointed out.

'Rest yourself, bro! He ain't gonna find out,' laughed Dean.

'That's really quite funny,' I said, giggling, as we moved off to our lesson.

'Me get famous!' said Dean as we walked into the classroom.

'You're gonna get killed, bro, is what you're gonna get,' smirked Jit.

'Shut up and sit down!' Mr Ashford shouted.

Dean grinned as we took our seats.

* * *

The next two weeks saw Imi, Hannah and Suky join up for the same clubs as Dean, Jit and I had joined. On Tuesdays we had Comics, Wednesdays was Chess, Thursdays, Book Club and Fridays, Computer Club. It was really good fun, all of us being together at lunch times and the clubs were actually quite interesting, apart from Chess which was just a laugh. And getting used to early lunch wasn't exactly hard to do. Even Imi and Suky, who had argued the most when I'd told them about the socials, came round and saw the benefits of joining up. I was just surprised that the whole school wasn't at it. Although that was probably a good thing because the more people that didn't know, the less chance there was of getting caught out.

No one seemed to care that we were all suddenly walking out of lessons ten minutes early. It was just accepted. The only teacher to raise a question had been Mr Herbert but then he was always suspicious of everything. Besides, the morning that we all left his English lesson he had this huge pus-filled boil on his forehead, and I think that he was too gutted to complain. I know that I would have been. He grunted something at us and Dean told him to chill out and get some antiseptic cream (under his breath though).

If we'd known how things were going to end up, I don't think any of us would have been laughing. You see, Dean's stinky song ruined everything and I even managed to get some of the blame. Can you believe that – little old me?

FIFTEEN

Our scam lasted for three more weeks before things started to go wrong. It was a Thursday when we began to run out of luck. We were all sitting in Mr Herbert's English lesson, clock-watching, waiting for the moment that we could leave. Every minute or so, Jit leaned across and asked me what time it was and in the end I got so wound up that I ignored him completely. Mr Herbert was in a really bad mood and I didn't want to get into trouble with him. Since the minute we had walked into the classroom, he'd had a face on him like a cow with a slapped bum. When he spoke it was through gritted teeth and he was all red in the face. Well, redder than usual anyway. As Hannah had once said, Mr Herbert hadn't been around when they'd passed out the good looks – he'd obviously been on the other side of the planet, running face first into parked cars or something. She was sure that he had some other positive qualities, only we were still waiting to find out what they were. On that day, his face was more screwed up than ever.

'He's got his face on inside out,' Jit joked in a whisper.

'Man must have constipation,' Dean whispered back.

It took all of my will power to resist laughing out loud, especially when Dean whispered that his grand-dad got constipation regularly, and pulled a face to mimic him.

'Serious, my gramps spent all his time looking like this . . . and then he'd say, "*Mi cyan pass mi stool, dem . . .*" Even at the dinner table he'd be tellin' us bout his problem, droolin' an' that.'

'Ssh!' I replied.

'Serious – he used to say that his poo was all hard and dry and that and could my mum put extra hot peppers in his curry so that he'd stay regu—'

'Urgh, Dean!' I said out loud, regretting it instantly.

'Grace Parkhurst – perhaps you'd be kind enough to tell us what you're talking to Mr Chambers about?' spat Herbert.

'Er . . .'

'I should say you've *erred,* young lady. Now shut up

and let me get on with teaching the people in this class who aren't arrogant enough to assume that they know everything already,' he told me.

I went bright red and tried to think up clever replies but decided that the silly man wasn't worth it. He was probably sad and lonely anyway, and who was I to pick on him and make his life any worse than it already was?

Herbert turned to his board and proceeded to write out a list of points about something. I didn't know what it was because I hadn't been paying attention and I had to lean across Jit, who wasn't even bothering to pretend to write something down, and copy what Hannah was writing. It had something to do with imagery in poems.

I looked at my watch. It was eleven fifteen. We had over half an hour before we could leave for Book Club. I decided that the best way to pass the time was to act-ually pay attention, which I managed to do until just past half eleven. Suddenly a grinning face appeared in the glass next to the door and the sound of chanting went up outside the classroom. It was muffled at first, because the door was closed, but slowly I began to make out the words as it got louder. Mr Herbert started turning purple with rage, trying to ignore it.

'*GEEZER'S 'AVIN A HEART ATTACK . . .!*' someone shouted, banging on the door.

I looked over at Dean, who was sitting with a grin on his face, and then Jit, who shook his head.

'Mi start a fashion,' beamed Dean, as someone opened the door.

Herbert shouted 'Oi!', his voice actually getting higher not lower. Some of the class began to laugh and you could see Herbert was about to go bananas.

The lad in the doorway ignored him and rapped some more. '*WITH YUH RED UP FACE AN DA HAIR YUH LACK, SOMETIMES YOU EVEN SMELL KINDA WACK!*'

Behind him were three or four of his mates and they began to shout 'Big Up Herbert – an' da Herbert Rap!' Mr Herbert started to shake and then he exploded, throwing his board marker at the lad in the doorway before chasing after all of them as they ran off down the stairwell laughing. Nearly everyone in the class ran to the door in a mad scramble, Jit and Dean at the head, sending chairs and desks and bits of paper flying everywhere. I stayed where I was with Imi, Suky and Hannah, shaking my head.

'Someone's in big trouble over this,' I told the others.

'Yeah – how can they just disrupt a lesson like that and get away with it?' replied Imi.

We sat and waited for about five minutes before the stampede returned, picking up the chairs they had knocked over and returning the desks to their original positions. Behind them came Mr Singh and Miss Khan, telling us all to quieten down and get back to what we were doing. I looked at my watch. It was quarter to twelve.

'Miss Khan?' I said before raising my hand in the air.

'Yes, Grace?' smiled Miss Khan, who was the prettiest teacher at Devana High by a mile and also one of the nicest.

'Some of us have got to go at ten to because of . . .'

'Oh right, yes . . . those who are part of the lunch thingy can go now,' she replied before I could finish, saving me from admitting to the whole class what we were up to. After all, it was our secret and I wanted to keep it that way.

As some of the other kids gave us a few looks, Mr Singh raised his eyebrows at Jit and Dean, following them out into the hallway.

'What's this?' he grinned. 'You two going to a social?'

'Er . . . yeah,' replied Jit, sheepishly.

'What?' grinned Dean. 'It's Book Club and my mum reckons it's worth it for my education,' he told Singh.

'I'm sure it is – I'm just surprised that's all. Surprised and a little proud too. It shows great initiative, lads,' Singh replied.

'Cheers, sir,' beamed Dean.

'What's going on down there, sir?' I asked Mr Singh.

'Never mind about that, Grace – just get to wherever you're going to, please,' he told me.

'Oh, sir!' I complained.

'Goodbye, Grace,' he replied, going back into the classroom.

'He's checkin' her – that Miss Khan,' said Jit to no one in particular, as we walked down the stairwell to the dinner hall.

'How'd you know?' Suky asked him.

'Singh and Khan? Man, that's just nasty,' said Imtiaz.

'Why is it?' asked Hannah. 'They're both about the

same age and they ain't exactly ugly the pair of 'em – I reckon they'd make a nice couple.'

'Yeah so do I,' agreed Suky.

'What you two bangin' on about?' dismissed Dean, waving his hand.

'Hey, check out what's going on over there!' whispered Jit, as we reached the main corridor at the foot of the stairs.

Across the corridor, in the opposite direction to the hall, stood Mr Black with Herbert, Granger and Wilson, all surrounding a lad called Paresh Solanki and his mates. They looked sheepish and I could tell that they were being lectured by Mr Black. We stood and watched for a moment.

'Move along please!' bellowed Mr Black when he saw us, his face red from the effort.

We turned and headed in the opposite direction, ready for hot food and big-time gossip. The social itself was taken up with discussing the stupidity of Paresh and his friends. Everyone knew about it, even the pupils that weren't in the lesson, but Devana High is like that – gossip takes no time to get round. We didn't bother talking about the list of five books that we were supposed to discuss, even though I'd read one of them and was desperate to tell the group what I thought about it. By the end of the club we hadn't talked about anything but what had happened during our lesson. Dean was still smiling as we walked to afternoon registration and continued to wear his silly grin into the next lesson. He was really proud that his rap had achieved cult status at Devana High. And you know what they say about pride coming before a fall . . .

SIXTEEN

The next morning we were sitting in Mr Granger's CDT lesson waiting to leave for early lunch. Jit and Dean were doing their usual routine, winding each other and the rest of us up, as Mr Granger ignored them. He offered the occasional 'Ssh!' but nothing more than that, which was strange. Normally he was the kind of teacher that would throw pupils out of his lesson for being disruptive. He was showing us the basics of using a saw, and then began to go through the different types of saw that were available. It was an introduction to woodworking and to a project which meant making our own spatulas. I was actually quite interested and every so often I nudged Dean, who was sitting next to me, only for him to ignore me and carry on teasing Jit about a spot that had appeared on the end of his nose. He was getting his own back big time.

'It's like a new head, man,' whispered Dean, as Jit tried to cover it up.

'Get lost!' he whispered back.

'Any minute now the thing's goin' to start talking to me,' continued Dean.

Jit picked up his pen and told Dean he was going to stab him with it but Dean just laughed. 'You might wanna use it to bust all the pus outta that meteorite on your nose, bro,' he said.

'Right!' bellowed Mr Granger, making me jump. 'I've had enough of you two!'

'At last,' whispered Suky. 'I thought he was never going to say anything.'

'Shut up and pay attention,' he told the lads, looking at his watch. 'You've only got five minutes before you go anyway – let's try and pay attention until then, hey?'

I looked at my watch which told me that it was only twenty-five minutes to twelve. I leaned across, behind Dean and Jit, and nudged Imtiaz.

'What time do you make it?' I whispered.

'Time you got a watch that works,' replied Imi, before looking at his own watch. 'Quarter to twelve.'

'Can't be,' I whispered back. 'Mine says that it's twenty-five to.'

'Like the man said,' Jit butted in, 'Get yourself a new watch.'

'OK,' came Mr Granger's voice. 'I've had enough of all of you. Get yourselves off to wherever it is that you go to on Friday lunch times.'

I looked at Dean, who looked at Jit, grinned and then stood up and made a big fuss of putting all his stationery into his bag. The rest of us followed suit and walked out of the classroom. I could have sworn that Mr Granger was smirking at us as we left. Not scowling, like he normally did when he was angry. But once we were on our way to the dining hall, I put it out of my mind. Why waste valuable brain power thinking about some stinky teacher and his facial expressions anyway?

The dinner hall was empty when we arrived. The dinner ladies were behind the counter chatting to each other and waiting for the rush to start. Normally there were one or two other pupils around, pupils like Wesley and Robert, other members of the lunch-club elite, only I couldn't see them. Jit and Dean ordered their daily helping of pizza and chips and I picked my sandwiches. The other three were already seated, and when we joined them, Imi was complaining about Dean.

'I wanted to learn something in that lesson,' he told Dean, as he sat down.

'Sorry, Dad,' replied Dean before stuffing half of his pizza slice into his mouth in one go.

'Seriously though,' added Hannah. 'Some of us actually want to learn and it doesn't help when you two mess about and get us thrown out.'

'What you on about?' mumbled Jit through a gob-full of chips.

'Jit! Can't you talk *after* you've swallowed your food?' said Suky in disgust.

'Yeah, that's just nasty,' I added in support.

Jit swallowed his mouthful and gave both of us a dirty look, before stuffing a load more in.

'We ain't stopping you from learning,' said Dean, defensively. He actually looked a little hurt, but Dean was a master at putting on faces so I ignored the slight pangs of guilt.

'Yes, actually you are,' I told him. 'I mean, I don't mind messing about – none of us do – but sometimes you have to pay attention.'

'Yeah – you two need to think about the rest of us for a change,' agreed Imtiaz.

'Sorry,' replied Dean, looking away.

'Don't be funny about it,' Hannah told him. 'It's not like we're accusing you of something you haven't done.'

'Yeah but you're saying me and Dean get you into trouble *all* the time – and we don't,' said Jit, after swallowing his food this time.

'Jit – you two are always getting us into trouble!' Imtiaz reminded him.

'*Yeah?*' asked Dean, aggressively. '*When?*'

'Like the time when you threw that *eraser* at Mrs Orton's head and blamed *me?*' said Hannah.

'Or the time you set *fire* to the text book in Maths with that lighter and we all got grief?' added Imtiaz.

'And what about that stuff with trying to get a free lunch because you said there were *hairs* in your food? You were pulling them out of your *own* head and putting them in the fish fingers, remember? And you blamed me!' Suky reminded him.

Dean tried to look hurt but couldn't. He broke into a grin and he laughed. 'Yeah but I was only messin' and that was ages ago,' he said through his laughter.

'We ain't got you in no trouble this year,' added Jit.

'*Woo-hoo!*' cried Hannah, sarcastically. 'You've grown up – break out the champagne.'

'Oh get lost, *Hannah Banana*,' replied Jit.

'Wow! Haven't heard that one since infant school,' smiled Hannah.

Jit grinned and finished his food. Dean had already scoffed his and the rest of us had sandwiches which we took with us to Computer Club. On the way Dean boasted about how his 'Herbert Rap' had become popular.

'Move over, people! Ah me run *tings* now!'

'You gonna be in trouble when he finds out it was you who made it up,' said Imtiaz.

'How's he gonna find out?' asked Dean as we entered the classroom where the club was held.

There were rows of PCs and screens but absolutely no other pupils. I looked out into the corridor and saw no one turning up behind us either. Strange.

'Looks like we got here early,' said Jit.

'Come on, let's look for pictures of naked celebrities on the internet,' grinned Dean.

'You can't, you little perv,' said Hannah. 'The search engines are blocked and anyway – this is a club for learning about how to use different bits of software – not searching the internet.'

Dean tried to connect to Google but a message box told him that the modem wasn't connected.

'That's so lame!' he said, opening up the paint box software and doodling on screen.

'What's that supposed to be?' I asked him, smiling at his inability to use the mouse like a paint brush.

'Your face, you cheeky monkey,' he replied, trying to draw out eyes, a nose and a mouth.

'*Charming*,' I said, pretending to pout.

'Why don't you try it then, Miss Artist? See if you can do any better.'

Dean moved over and I pulled a chair up, sitting down and taking hold of the mouse. There were still no other pupils. I deleted Dean's lame effort and began to paint out a face, using different colours.

'Man – you never said that you knew how to use it!' he complained.

'My dad uses it every day, well, a form of it anyway,' I reminded him. 'And you didn't ask, did you?'

'*You're so clever – can I be your friend?*' asked Dean in a stupid voice.

I was just about to reply in a stupid voice of my own when the door opened and Mr Black greeted us with a beaming smile.

'Good afternoon, pupils,' he said.

'Hi, Mr Black,' smiled Hannah.

'Now let me see,' replied Mr Black, smiling back. 'This would be your . . . Oh I guess this would be your fourth lunch time social this week, wouldn't it?'

My mouth dropped open just before everyone else's did the same. I could feel myself beginning to go bright red.

'We're in the dog whatsit now!' whispered Jit.

'Indeed, Mr Kooner,' answered the principal, still smiling, as he was joined by Mr Herbert, Mrs Lee-Cross, Mr Granger and a very disappointed-looking Mrs Dooher . . .

SEVENTEEN

'It seems to me that we have a problem,' said Mr Black, sitting on a desk next to Imtiaz.

Mrs Dooher looked at me. Mr Herbert was wearing a self-satisfied look and the other teachers just stood there. I tried to hold Mrs Dooher's eyes but started to feel embarrassed and a little bit guilty, like I had let her down, so I looked away. Jit and Dean sat in silence, heads down.

'Would you like to explain things, Mr Dhondy?' the principal asked Imtiaz.

'Er . . .' he began, trying to find the right words to say.

'How about you, Miss Kaur?' asked Mr Black, looking at Suky. She turned her eyes towards Dean and Jit, saying nothing.

'We didn't realize . . .' began Jit, about to lie through his teeth. Big mistake.

'Don't lie, Kooner!' snapped Herbert, his face reddening. 'We're well aware of what's been going on.'

Jit glared at Herbert. I closed my eyes and prayed that he wouldn't do anything to make things worse. I had this funny feeling in my stomach, the kind of feeling you get when you feel frightened. I began to wonder just how much trouble we were in.

'The funny thing is,' said Mr Black, 'if you hadn't stopped to gawp at Paresh Solanki's misfortune, I doubt we would have noticed you. And if Mr Solanki hadn't kindly informed us of Dean's little rap, we might not have had a conversation about your little group.'

Everyone turned to look at Dean, who was squirming in his chair. I gulped down air.

'And had we not had the conversation that we did we might not have realized that you've been going to far too many lunch clubs,' continued Mr Black.

'Unfortunate coincidence,' smiled Mr Herbert. 'For you.'

'Although I almost *admire* your initiative,' continued Mr Black, 'I'm afraid that you have broken the rules and as such you will have to face the consequences. You know me – firm but fair, people. *Firm but fair.*'

Imi groaned and muttered that it wasn't *his* fault.

'Then perhaps you'd like to point out the person or persons responsible for this little episode?' snapped Mr Herbert again.

Imtiaz caught my eye and then looked at Dean and Jit. He waited for a moment and then shook his head.

'No – it was all of us,' he said.

'All of you?' questioned Mr Herbert. 'Not one or two of you leading the rest astray?'

'No!' burst out Hannah. 'We all did it together!'

'*Really?* Past form suggests that there's usually a couple of ringleaders amongst you,' replied Herbert, looking at Dean and Jit with his beady little eyes.

'Actually,' I said, allowing the stupid part of my brain to win over the goody two-shoes bit, 'it was my idea.'

Mr Herbert sniggered.

'Forgive me if I find that unbelievable,' he sneered.

'Forgive you for your face, more like,' mumbled Dean.

'I'm sorry, Mr Chambers,' replied Mr Black. 'Is there something you wish to say?'

'No,' said Dean, looking up at me.

'It *was* me!' I said in a loud voice. 'I told them all about it.'

'We all joined in,' added Suky. 'So it's down to all of us.'

Mr Black shook his head. Then he turned to Dean. 'Your form tutor will inform you of your punishment. And Mr Chambers, if you'd like to come and pay me a visit in my office afterwards, please.'

'But that's not fair . . .' I began.

'Oh yes it is, young lady,' answered Mr Black. 'Firm. But fair.'

With his motto still ringing in our ears, he got up and strode out of the room. Mrs Dooher stayed but the other three followed the leader. She closed the door behind Mrs Lee-Cross and turned to face us.

'You are a bunch of idiots,' she said in a soft voice.

'But miss—' began Jit.

'I'm not interested,' replied Mrs Dooher. 'You've put me in a very tricky position. How exactly do I explain that six members of my form group broke the rules together?'

'Ain't your fault, is it?' said Dean.

'No, Dean. From what I can tell it's yours,' she answered.

'Yeah!' snapped Imtiaz. 'Cheers, Dean. You've got us all into trouble again.'

'No one held no gun to your head, did they?' Jit snapped back.

'If he hadn't gone on about it,' said Suky, before looking at me, 'we wouldn't have been tempted, would we? And let's not forget Grace either.'

'Oh go and boil your head,' I said, meaning to lighten the situation, only Suky took it the wrong way and got angry with me.

'Get stuffed, you cow!' she shouted.

'SHUT UP!'

We all looked at Mrs Dooher in surprise. I don't think that I had ever heard her shout before. I sensed that Jit was about to break into a grin and I desperately tried to get his attention by kicking his chair but he ignored me and smiled.

'Wow, miss is getting—' he began.

'I mean it, Jit,' said Mrs Dooher. 'You've let me down very badly. I thought that you had more intelligence than this . . . It was a very stupid thing to do. You know it took the combined efforts of myself, Mrs Lee-Cross and Mr Granger to persuade Mr Black not to cancel all the socials for the rest of the year.'

'But that's just stupid,' said Dean. 'Why should everyone else suffer just 'cos we messed up?'

'*Exactly*, Dean,' replied Mrs Dooher. 'The socials are there so that you can learn new things, not skive off lessons and get early lunches every day. The clubs are an extra curricular activity. The school doesn't *have* to run them.'

'We know, miss,' said Hannah. 'We *are* sorry.'

'That's beside the point, I'm afraid,' said Mrs Dooher.

'So what's he gonna do to us then?' asked Jit.

'Mr Herbert wanted the book thrown at you but Mrs Lee-Cross persuaded Mr Black that there was an alternative.'

'What is it, miss?' asked Suky.

'Yeah – what has this *fool* got us into this time?' added Imtiaz.

'Who you calling *fool*, pretty bwoi?' snapped Dean.

'*You*, you fool.'

'Shut it!' shouted Mrs Dooher. 'I don't care whose fault it is – all of you made a choice to break the rules and deceive your teachers.'

'That's a bit harsh innit, miss? It ain't like we killed

someone and buried 'em under the tennis courts,' said Jit.

We all turned to look at him, the weirdo, and even Mrs Dooher nearly broke out a grin.

'You strange child,' laughed Hannah, shaking her head.

'Wha'?' asked Jit, shrugging his shoulders.

'It's a breach of trust,' said Mrs Dooher. 'And trust is a very important thing. Now you lot are going to have to re-earn mine and that of the rest of the staff.'

Imi groaned again.

'So, let me tell you what's going to happen. On Mondays, Tuesdays and Wednesdays, for the rest of the term, you're all going to help out in the dinner hall, clearing tables and emptying plates.'

'NO WAY!' shouted Jit, getting a seriously dirty look from Mrs Dooher. A look that could kill. But she didn't stop to tell him off.

'. . . and you'll have late lunches on those days too. And on Thursdays and Fridays, you'll attend extra Maths tutorials, with work set for you.'

'For the whole term?' moaned Suky.

'Yeah – talk about overreacting, miss,' added Hannah. 'The punishment is supposed to fit the crime, isn't it?'

'Let me finish,' replied Mrs Dooher. 'There will be an opportunity to shorten the period of punishment. If Mr Black feels that you *aren't* trying to slack off during your punishment, and Mrs Lee-Cross sees a marked improvement in your attitudes towards Maths, then they'll review the situation . . . in two weeks' time.'

'Great,' snapped Imtiaz.

'Well I ain't doin it,' said Jit, sullenly.

'I'm afraid that you are, Jit,' replied Mrs Dooher, softly.

'But it ain't fair,' he said.

'And nor is what you did.'

Dean, who had been quiet for a while, slid his chair back and stood up.

'I'm going to see the top dog,' he told Mrs Dooher, not bothering to wait for her permission.

'Dean!' Mrs Dooher called out but he ignored her, slamming the door and swearing at the top of his voice in the corridor.

'He'll be OK, miss,' said Hannah. 'He's just letting off steam.'

'I know,' she replied with a tired smile. 'I just hope that he lets it all off before he reaches Mr Black's office.'

'We're really sorry,' I said, as much to the others as to Mrs Dooher.

'And very stupid,' she replied. 'Now get outside with the rest of the pupils.'

I tried to talk to Imtiaz and Suky as we walked down the stairs and out of the doors that led to the tennis courts, but they both told me to go away.

When I approached Hannah, she told me that she had to talk to someone about homework and walked off towards a group of girls from her old school. Jit had gone off in a sulk too, so I sat on my own and wondered what I was going to do to make it up to my friends . . .

EIGHTEEN

The brainwave hit me on Saturday morning, in the checkout queue at Sainsbury's with my dad, as he tried to find his wallet.

'I'm sure it's here somewhere,' he said to the man behind us, apologetically.

'Dad – I've got something I need to tell you,' I said, wondering if it was a good moment to remind him that he'd given me his wallet for safekeeping. It was in my little shoulder bag which hung at my side.

'Not now, Grace,' he said, as the checkout operator smiled at us and said hello.

'But it's really important,' I said, beginning to unload the trolley's contents onto the conveyor belt. As the bar codes on each item of shopping beeped past the red light, I opened my bag and took out his wallet.

'I think it might be in the car,' said my dad absent-mindedly. 'I'll just nip out and see . . .'

'Dad – it's here. You gave it to me in the cheese aisle because it fell out of your back pocket.' I handed it to him and put more stuff on the belt.

'Ah! There it is,' he said, as though it had just appeared out of thin air. Like maybe the air in his head.

'Dad?'

'OK, Grace – what do you want to tell me?' he relented.

'I . . . we got into trouble at school yesterday.'

My dad smiled at the woman on the checkout and then turned to me.

'Who do you mean by "we", and what trouble exactly?' he asked. Looking worried.

'It's nothing much . . . just silly stuff and all of us got into trouble.'

'What – even Suky and Imtiaz?'

'Yes,' I replied. Even my dad knew that those two were perfect. Supposedly.

'And I thought they were such mature young people,' he said, trying not to smile.

'It's not funny, Dad – me and Dean got everyone else into trouble and they won't talk to me now and I don't know what to do about it.'

'Can you start packing this stuff?' asked my dad.

'Are you listening to me?'

'Yes, Grace, I am. I just want you to pack whilst you talk, that's all.'

As I packed the shopping, I told him all about what had happened. Everything – no leaving bits out or anything. Dad didn't look at me once as I talked and, when I'd finished, he just pocketed his wallet and said goodbye to the checkout woman. Convinced he'd been ignoring me, I went into a sulk. My dad saw me push out my bottom lip and smiled as he pushed the trolley, now full of bags filled to bursting point, out of the store.

'I heard everything,' he said. 'I just don't know what you want me to do about it, that's all.'

'I've got an idea – something that I need your help with over the weekend.'

Dad raised an eyebrow.

'What exactly?' he asked.

'Something that will get my friends talking to me again and make up for what me and Dean got them into.'

We were at the car by that point and Dad patted his pockets, hoping to hear the jangle of car keys. When he didn't get it, he started to look panicked.

'Damn!' he said. 'I must have left them at the till.'

Before I could reply, he walked off towards the store again, so I didn't get the chance to tell him that I also had his car keys. I could have gone after him. Shouted even. But I decided to let him go, smiling to myself at the thought of him asking if anyone had seen his keys and then thinking that he had lost them. I got the keys out, opened the doors and started to load the bags into the boot.

'Very funny . . .' he said, grinning when he returned. 'Although your mother might not see it that way – I've just called her from the store and asked her to bring me the spares.'

'You've got to call her back,' I said in a panic of my own. 'She was going to have a lie-in and . . .' The thought of my mum having to get up early after a really hectic week at work didn't appeal to me. She'd be moody and I'd get it in the neck for playing my trick. I was in enough trouble as it was.

'Only kidding, Grace,' he replied.

'*Dad!*'

There was a bunch of deep-red grapes sitting on top of one of the shopping bags and I plucked one from the rest and threw it at his head. He ducked and the grape flew on, straight into the back of some woman's head. I got into the car as she turned and gave my dad a filthy look. He smiled and shrugged his shoulders before getting in and trying to tell me off through his laughter. Then, on the way home, I filled him in on my idea.

Dean was standing at the bus stop the following Monday morning as my dad pulled up to the curb. I lowered the window and told him to get in.

'So what – we getting chauffeur driven to school today?' he asked, getting in.

It was a cold morning and Dean shivered as the car heater warmed him up.

'Thanks, Mr Parkhurst,' he said.

'It's totally *cool*, bro,' replied my dad, trying, yet *again*, to act like he was a teenager.

'Dad!' I said, giggling.

'Nah, Grace,' laughed Dean. 'Mr Parkhurst is cool.'

'Thanks, Dean,' beamed my dad as he turned up the latest hip hop CD that *I'd* told him to buy.

'Wicked!' grinned Dean. 'Man could get *used* to this, y'know.'

'I don't think so,' I said.

'You got that thing you were telling me about on the phone?' asked Dean, remembering what I'd told him on Sunday.

'Yeah!'

I opened my bag and gave him a look at my brain-child.

'*Yes, Sister Gee – ah you dat!*' said Dean, nodding his head to the beat.

I think he was trying to say I was clever or talented or something but I didn't actually know. And I was too cool to admit that sometimes I didn't have a clue what he was on about. He'd only tease me forever if I did.

Mr Black was at the front gate as my dad walked us both in.

'Ah, Mr Parkhurst – good morning,' beamed Mr Black. 'And good morning to you two – bright and early, I see.'

'Good morning, Mr Black,' replied my dad.

'Hi, sir,' I said.

Dean mumbled a quick hello and shot off towards the doors.

'Do we have a meeting scheduled, Mr Parkhurst?' asked my principal, looking confused.

'No – we don't. I'm here on the off-chance that you can spare me half an hour or so of your *valuable* time.'

'A school matter?' asked Mr Black.

'Yes,' my dad told him.

'Of course, sir. How can I be of service?'

For a moment I thought that he was going to bow or something, but he didn't. He asked my dad to go and take a seat in reception, and said that he'd be along in a minute or two. I walked my dad into the foyer and signed him in before taking him to the waiting area outside Mr Black's huge, untidy office. I sat down with him and watched the other pupils go by, all of them staring at my dad and me, wondering what was going on. Usually when someone's parents sat with them outside the principal's office, they were in serious trouble.

About five minutes after we had sat down, Mr Black walked up, his infamous detention list clipped to the board that hung at his side. He grinned and said that he'd take it from there, and told me to get off to registration.

'Oh, I'm sorry,' smiled Dad. 'I forgot to say that Grace would be joining us. That's not a problem, is it?'

'Not at all, Mr Parkhurst,' replied Mr Black, genuinely. 'Perhaps I can get you both a cup of coffee?'

'That would be lovely,' said Dad, as we were ushered into the office and asked to sit down. Mr Black lifted his phone and asked someone on the other end for three coffees. He put the phone down and then turned to me and my dad.

'So what seems to be the problem?' he asked.

My dad told him what we had been doing all weekend. Then he explained that although he thought that the gang deserved to be punished, he hoped that it might be something constructive.

'Something firm but fair, Mr Black,' he said, without any hint of a smile, the cheeky monkey.

'I totally agree. You say that you've prepared one in advance?' asked Mr Black, his eyes gleaming with what looked like excitement.

'Yes!' I chirped up for the first time, feeling more confident. I opened my bag and got out my brainchild, handing it to Mr Black. He looked amazed.

'And this can be done using ordinary software?'

'Yes,' replied Dad. 'Software that I'm going to donate to the school as a show of goodwill.'

'And you're willing to come in and train the students and staff on usage, troubleshooting, that sort of thing?'

'Absolutely. I thought maybe four lunch times this week – perhaps beginning tomorrow?'

'Marvellous!' bellowed Mr Black. 'If only some of the other parents were able to show such an interest.'

'So you'll let us do this *instead*?' I asked him, wanting to be sure.

'Absolutely, Grace,' he replied. 'Just think of the benefits for the school.'

'So we *don't* have to do the extra Maths and clear up the dining hall . . .?' I said, pushing it.

'No – but I do think that you should forfeit early lunches. What do you think, Mr Parkhurst?'

'Call me Michael,' replied Dad, smiling. 'And yes, I think that's very appropriate.'

He looked at me and winked. I winked back. Well you can't win them all and I *had* got the gang out of the other stuff.

'Perhaps Grace could get along to her lesson and leave us to discuss the details?' asked Mr Black, looking excited again.

'OK,' I said, kissing Dad on the cheek and thanking Mr Black again.

'You know my motto,' smiled the principal.

'Yes, sir – firm but fair.'

'Exactly, Grace. And may I say that I admire your initiative.'

'Thank you, sir,' I replied, beaming as I made my way to what was left of my first lesson.

NINETEEN

Mr Black waited until lunch time to get us all together. I had a hard time keeping my secret to myself. I was gagging to tell someone else. Only Suky, Imi and Hannah were still upset and not talking to me, so that made it a little easier. And I had just as hard a time convincing Dean to keep quiet too. He wanted to tell Jit, who had spent all morning threatening to skive off when the dinner bell went. Dean didn't want him to get into even more trouble.

It was ten minutes to twelve when a Year Seven pupil walked into our classroom with a message from the principal. Mr Woods, our History teacher, read the note and then called out our names, one by one.

'It seems that you have an audience with Mr Black,' he told us, smiling. 'I wonder what that could be about?'

'Sack that,' whispered Jit. 'I'm outta here.'

Suky, Hannah and Imi groaned and got their things together, trudging off to Mr Black's office without waiting for the rest of us. I got up quickly and followed, telling Jit to hurry up. When we got out of the classroom I told Jit that he *had* to come with us to see Mr Black.

'Why?' he asked, stubbornly.

'Because he's got something to tell us,' I replied.

'He ain't got nothin' to say to me that I'm interested in,' said Jit.

'He's letting us off,' I said.

'What?'

'He's not making us do the dinner hall thing. We're going to be doing something else instead,' said Dean.

'Yeah – bet it's even worse,' he replied, unconvinced.

'My dad will be there,' I said, knowing that it would change his mind.

'Your old man? In Mr Black's office?'

I grinned. 'Yeah,' I said. 'Come on!'

'But why is your dad here?' asked Jit.

'Patience, boy,' I told him, putting on a posh voice. 'It's not good to pester a lady for her secrets. And I *am* a *lady!*'

'This better be good,' replied Jit.

'Shut up, you girl, and get a move on,' Dean told him.

As we walked into Mr Black's office, the others were waiting for us, looking moody. My dad was sitting where I had left him, a cup of coffee in front of him on Mr Black's desk and a couple of sheets of notes too. Mr Black waited for me to close the door before he spoke.

'Well, it seems as though you've had a slight reprieve,' he told us.

'I don't understand,' said Hannah.

'I . . . we've decided to give you something else to do during the dinner hour,' continued Mr Black, acknowledging my dad.

Suky and Imi both gave me a funny look. I smiled at them.

'Rather than make you do what I proposed on Friday, I've been convinced to let you participate in a little school history. From tomorrow Mr Parkhurst is going to use the lunch hour to instruct you all on the usage of a piece of design software, in order that you can produce, monthly . . .'

He coughed for effect and went over to his desk to

pick up my brainchild. Turning round, he showed it to the others. Hannah gasped and Suky and Imtiaz just looked at each other.

'. . . *The Devana High Telegraph.* Our own school newspaper.'

He held out the four-page newspaper that my dad and I had put together over the weekend.

'But . . .' began Jit.

'But nothing, young man. You will participate or you will carry out the previous punishment.'

'No, it ain't that,' said Jit. 'I just don't get it. What about punishing us?'

'Well, you will have to go for late lunch for the rest of the term,' answered Mr Black, 'so there is still an element of punishment. It's just that I've been convinced to give all of you a second chance. A chance to contribute to this school and to give something to its pupils. I should think that you'd all be very pleased.'

Hannah looked at me and grinned.

'Thank you, sir,' she told Mr Black, and beamed.

'Yeah,' agreed Imtiaz. 'Thanks, sir.'

'Don't thank me, people. It was all Grace's idea and she was helped by her father. If you're going to thank anyone, it should be them.'

'And Dean,' I told them. 'Dean helped me with it too.'

I looked at my dad and winked on the sly. Dean looked confused but he didn't bother to point out my little white lie. He just scratched his head and then smiled a bit.

'It won't be a chance to skive, mind,' added Mr Black. 'You'll be supervised and I expect to see the paper go from strength to strength over the coming year. And of course I'll expect you all to train other pupils too . . .'

I stood where I was and smiled a big, fat, wide smile as Mr Black outlined what he wanted in the paper. Soon the others were asking him questions and telling my dad what they thought should go into the first issue. Imi and Dean wanted to do a sports section and Suky asked if she could write a gossip column. Hannah applied for the post of Editor and Writer-in-Chief, cementing her status as bum-lick by offering to do the first feature on Mr Black himself.

'You know,' Dean said to him as we left his office to go for lunch, 'you're all right really. Like people say that you're *too* strict and that but I reckon you is OK, bro. Firm but fair, know what I mean?'

Mr Black grinned, either not getting that Dean was having a joke at his expense, or just not caring. We went off to lunch and Suky, Imtiaz and Hannah all said they were sorry as we stood in the queue for soggy sandwiches. I told them that I was cool with it all and really looking forward to starting on the newspaper. We collected our excuse for lunches and went to sit down, followed by Dean and Jit.

'Your dad's really lovely,' said Suky. 'Helping us all out like that.'

'Are you kidding?' I replied. 'The minute I told him that I needed his help to design a newspaper he dragged me off to get the correct software package and teach-yourself manual. He's nuts. Lovely. But totally nuts.'

Dean and Jit joined us and began to shovel the food down as usual.

'These chips are like concrete,' grinned Dean.

'Pure nasty,' agreed Jit, picking one up and throwing it over his head, not looking to see who was behind him.

'Oi!' came a familiar high pitched shout. It was Mr Herbert.

Dean and Jit didn't move. They carried on

eating and talking as though Mr Herbert didn't exist.

'I'm talking to you two,' he shouted.

Jit turned round and smiled at him.

'What?' he asked.

'Did you just throw this chip at me?' asked Herbert.

'No,' replied Jit, still smiling.

'Well, *someone* did.'

'Did you *see* me throw a chip?' asked Jit.

'That's not the point, is it?' said Mr Herbert.

'Maybe it fell from the sky?' said Dean.

'Yeah – out of that plane that takes all the Devana High leftovers to starving people in Africa,' suggested Jit.

Mr Herbert struggled to stay calm.

'And shouldn't the lot of you be clearing this mess up?' he asked, trying to change the subject.

'Actually,' I replied, 'Mr Black has given us something *much* more important to do.'

'*Ask* him if you don't believe us,' added Suky. 'He's in his office talking to Grace's *dad*.'

Mr Herbert mumbled something and went back to his dinner as Dean continued to moan.

'Nasty food, bro. Concrete chips . . . there's got to be a way to get out of late lunches, bro.'

We all stopped what we were doing and looked at him.

'What?' he asked.

'Shut up, Dean!' we all said together.

'Maybe there's another way out of it?' he continued.

One by one we all stood up and cleared our places, leaving Dean sitting on his own. But he didn't join us. Instead he turned to some girls from a different class in our year and started on them.

'Now, ladies . . . don't you think that it's unfair that we have to eat cold food and that?'

I giggled at him on my way out of the hall. Stinky boy. Jit came up beside me and asked me what I was doing later.

'Nothing – why don't you come over and we can have a snog,' I said, joking.

Jit looked startled. 'Relax, I was only kidding,' I added.

'Yeah until you get to Year Ten,' said Hannah, winking at me.

'You what?' asked Jit.

'Nothing . . .' I replied, kicking Hannah gently on the shin.

'Oi!'

'Oh shut up, you girl!' I said, smiling.

Jit looked at us both and shook his head. I smiled sweetly and linked arms with Hannah. Then we skipped out onto the tennis courts together as Jit looked on.

Maybe I'll snog him in Year Ten, I thought to myself, as I skipped along. *Maybe. If* he's wearing his lucky pants that is . . .

DEAN

*Once again to my Judgemeadow peeps 1983–1988,
especially Parmy, Penny, Ben, Lucy, Lisa Crouch,
Nina S, Veena, Esther, Hattie, Paul Williams, Phil
and Jez and the rest of the little gits, Gary Belle,
Gary Charles, Hilroy Thomas, everyone in CM
class over the five years, As, and anyone else that
I've not mentioned. With big love . . .*

ONE

'Dean!'

I shot up out of bed and shouted down to my mum that I was awake. Then I opened my bedroom door to see if the bathroom was free. It was. I picked up my towel and some underwear and ran for the shower before Ruby, my stupid older sister, could get in before me. Ruby spends hours in the bathroom, doing stuff that girls do, and I had to get to school. I didn't have no time for her nonsense. I had money to make.

'I'm off to work,' I heard my mum shout as I closed the bathroom door.

Five minutes into my shower I heard a familiar banging noise. 'Dean! Get your skinny ass outta there!'

It was Ruby. I had nearly finished anyway but I stood under the warm spray for another five minutes just to get on her nerves. It was my purpose in life – winding her up – and I was good at it.

When I got downstairs my older brother, Gussie, was already at the table, eating his breakfast.

'Yes, rude bwoi,' he said, grinning so that I could see the cornflake that was stuck to one of his manky teeth.

'Mornin', bro,' I replied, going into the kitchen to get a cup of tea and some toast.

My granddad was in there before me and he winked as he gave me a mug. 'Thanks, Gramps,' I said to him.

'Nuh worry yuhself, my yout',' he replied in his thick Jamaican accent.

'Any chance you could make me some toast an' all?' I asked, pushing my luck.

'Ounno mek yuh own dyam toas', yuh likkle spratt,' he told me. It took me a minute but in the end I worked out that he was saying 'no'.

'OK, Gramps,' I replied, shoving two slices of bread into the machine.

'An' get yuh batty ta school, man.'

I told him that I was trying to, but he just shook his head, mumbled something that I couldn't hear and left the kitchen. The toast popped out of the machine and I grabbed it, looking for a plate.

Back in the living room I sat down at the table and spread a thick layer of butter on my toast.

'Easy with that,' Gussie told me. 'That thing there will clog up yer heart, y'know.'

'It's only butter, man. It's natural.'

'Yeah – naturally full up of *fat*.'

I took a big bite of toast, chewed twice and swallowed. I followed that with a giant slurp of tea.

'Since when you cared about bein' healthy?' I asked my brother.

'I been goin' to the gym in town . . . weights and that.'

'About time too, yuh fat raas.'

I ducked as a table mat sailed over my head, shoved the rest of the piece of toast in my mouth and chewed it down fast. When I'd finished, I left my plate on the table and went to find my rucksack, passing my sister on the stairs.

'Man – that was quick. You showered *already*?' I asked her. She looked at me like I had something strange growing out of my nose.

'I just cleaned my teeth. I ain't like you,' she replied. 'How can you get yourself clean with only five minutes in the shower?'

'Is only so many times I can wash my bits,' I told her.

'I don't even want to *hear* it,' Ruby replied, holding her hand in my face.

I found my bag in my bedroom and ran back downstairs and into the living room.

'Who's gonna pick up your dishes after you?' asked Ruby.

I ignored her.

'You got them things for me?' I asked Gussie.

'Yeah – in that Asda bag on the sofa,' he replied.

I picked it up and looked inside where there were about thirty PlayStation games, all of them copies.

'How much each?' I asked.

'Tenner . . . and you can keep a quid each,' he replied.

I nodded and made for the door as Ruby got mad.

'I ain't your *slave*!' she shouted at the closing door. Not that I heard her say it. I just knew that she would.

My brother, Gussie, is eighteen, five years older than me. He buys and sells things and works behind the bar in my dad's place. He's supposed to be getting a proper job or doing a college course but it always gets put off. My dad thinks he'll get himself sorted out when he's good and ready. I know better. Gussie is a lazy, fat git and he'll sponge off my parents for as long as he can get away with it. His full name is Augustus Pablo Chambers. He's named after one of my parents' favourite reggae artists. I could laugh at him but my name is even worse. Dean Barrington Levy Chambers. I'm also named after a reggae artist, as is my sister. Oh and my dad. It runs in the family, I guess. Ruby's seventeen and her middle name is Lorna, after Lorna Bennett, who was a singer in the 1970s, and my dad is called Clement, after some bloke who ran Studio One Records in Jamaica, according to Gramps. In fact only Gramps and my mum have names that aren't linked to some Jamaican music person or other. Mum's name is Pearl and Gramps is called Ernest Theophilus Beresford Chambers. Or at least that's what it says on his passport. He's just Gramps at home.

Mum works at the city council. She's high up in some department or other. I don't have a clue what she actually does. She tried to tell me one time and it was so boring that I ended up watching some antiques programme on the TV for fun. It was *that* boring. My dad's got a cool job though. He owns a bar restaurant place in town and doesn't usually get up until after ten in the morning. Whenever my form teacher, Mrs

Dooher, tells me off for being late, I tell her that it runs in the family. Being late won't stop me from being great, I tell her. Seen? Only she never has a clue what I'm saying half the time. Still, she is like fifty or something. Lovely with it though.

Every morning since I met him at primary school, I call for my best mate, Jit. He lives down a side street off Evington Road, opposite the one my family live on, and most times he'll be waiting outside his front door for me. He won't walk down to the main road to make things easier. And he doesn't wait in his front room for me to get there before coming out, which is what I would do. Nah, he just stands there, on the pavement, looking like the nutter that he is. This morning though he wasn't there, and I thought that he was bunking off school again. He does that sometimes, a couple of days here and there when no one sees him. I don't know why and he never tells me, but then again I don't really ask. That 'let's talk about everything' stuff is for girls, anyway. My man will tell me when him good and ready.

I walked up to his front door, which needed a serious lick of paint, and knocked. The bell stopped working a couple of years ago and his mum, who he lives with, has never had it fixed. His dad lives on the other side of town and he never sees Jit. Something to do with family honour and stuff that I don't get. I call it the 'Asian ting' whenever it comes up, which is like once a year maybe. I'm sure he'll tell me about it properly, one of these days. I waited for Jit to answer and gave him a minute, tops. Usually if he hasn't answered by then, I'm gone. In sixty seconds, like in that lame film. I'd counted to twenty-five when he answered, looking all shady.

'Easy, Dean,' he said, opening the door.

'*Yes, bro!* An' isn't it a lovely *bright* mornin' too?' I replied, mimicking our headmaster, Mr Black.

Jit just shrugged at me and edged out of the gap in the door, like opening it fully would have set off an explosion or something.

'You have dead bodies hidden in there?' I asked as a joke.

'I could hide your dead body . . .' he told me, not even smiling. Weirdo.

We set off on our twenty minute walk to the *wrong* side of town, to go and wait for the bus. We always caught the same one, down by our friend Grace's house, even though we could get one nearer, on

Evington Road, to take us to school. I don't even *remember* why we started doing it, but it's like a tradition now and I wouldn't feel right if we didn't walk all that way. By the time we reached the top though, Grace was already gone, or so we thought, and we had to amuse ourselves by winding up a couple of lads from school, Robert Sargeant and Wesley Magoogan. They were talking about some new fantasy book and I *had* to join in.

'. . . and of course Gerafaggan is the *evil* one, the dark lord,' Robert was saying.

I looked at Jit and grinned.

'What kind of *name* is that?' I asked.

Robert and Wesley looked at me like I was missing my head.

'But he's a character from *The Dark Lord of Hazelwitch*,' replied Wesley, like I was supposed to know what that was. They could have been making it up for all I cared.

'It's really very *good*,' added Robert.

'Yeah but has it got talking animals and that?' I asked.

'Erm . . . yes, I believe it has,' Robert told me.

'There's a giant rat called Tar too – that's *rat* spelled

backwards by the way,' said Wesley, getting really excited.

'Hey, Fartyfartkins the Smelly or whatever yer name is – I look *stupid* to you?' I replied. 'Like, is *tar* really *rat* spelled *backwards*?'

Wesley looked down at his feet.

'Any fit women in it?' asked Jit.

'I think that rather depends on your imagination,' Robert told him. 'Of course in one's head a character takes on the features that one would *like* to give them.'

Jit just scratched his head and looked puzzled.

'He means that you can make the woman look like who you want, bruv,' I explained.

'I *knew* that,' lied Jit.

'In my head,' began Wesley, 'Princess Wondlebarn is actually rather similar to Catwoman.'

'Yes, and in my head there's a little hammer striking against the nerves, telling me that this conversation has reached its *nadir*,' I replied.

Wesley and Robert looked at each other and carried on their discussion. Jit shook his head.

'I bet that's all you do – look up words in a dictionary all night.'

'Least I can read,' I said.

'What's it mean, anyway?' he asked, as a familiar estate car pulled up alongside the bus stop and Grace smiled at us.

'It means like the end. The lowest point of any particular thing.'

'I swear you're turning into one of *them*!' Jit said to me, as we opened the car door and got in. He didn't tell me who '*them*' were though.

Grace turned round and gave us a big smile.

'My two favourite smelly pants,' she said.

'Easy, Sister Gee,' I replied.

'Yeah . . . er . . . hello,' added Jit, giving Grace this funny look. It's a look he often gives her and I think it means that he likes her but he isn't sure how to make it obvious. But he doesn't need to anyway. Everyone except him and Grace know that they fancy each other. He should just ask her out, I reckon.

Her dad turned and smiled too.

'Hello, lads – how are we this morning. *Kickin'* or *stink*, as you young 'uns like to say?'

'*Dad!*' said Grace, getting embarrassed, like she always does when he tries to pretend he's cool.

'We're good, Mr Parkhurst,' I replied.

'Yeah, we're chilling,' agreed Jit.

'Excellent – and call me Michael, please.'

He pushed a button on the stereo and a load of trumpet nonsense blasted out of the speakers.

'Miles Davis,' he told us as we drove off.

'Got his *every* CD,' I muttered, having a laugh, even though I actually quite liked it. Not that I was going to tell Grace's dad.

TWO

Mr Black was waiting at the school gates as Grace's dad parked up and let us out. Normally Black would have told us off for being late, but he just smiled at us before talking to Grace's dad for a bit.

'Good morning, Michael!' he boomed in his deep voice as we made our way into school.

'Your dad and Black are like best mates,' Jit told Grace.

'No they're not,' replied Grace, looking all sheepish.

'Best thing, I reckon,' I told them.

'Why is that, then?' asked Jit.

'It's like he's on our side and that,' I told him. 'We get into trouble and Mr Parkhurst can help us out – like he did with them lunch time clubs.'

I was talking about a scam that had backfired a few weeks earlier. I had convinced my friends that we should join these boring social clubs that run at lunch time, just so that we wouldn't have to have late lunches. Only we went a bit far and got into trouble. Grace's dad saved us though.

'He won't do that all the time,' said Grace.

'Would if *you* asked him,' I told her.

'Why would I do that, smelly pants?' she replied.

''Cos you love us,' I said.

Jit gave me a funny look, like I was trying it on or something. I just shook my head at him.

'Don't get your panties in a—' I began.

'GET TO YOUR FORM ROOMS!' boomed another familiar voice. It was Mr Herbert, one of the English teachers and Enemy No. 1.

'That's what we're doin',' replied Jit.

'Not fast enough,' snapped Herbert.

'You want us to run?' I asked him.

'Run and fall *over* and break a bone or two?' added Grace. 'Then we'd *have* to go to hospital and the doctors would ask us what happened and *we'd* say that *you* told us to run and then my dad would *have* to sue the school and it would all just end up in a *terrible* mess . . .'

'Shut it, Grace, and get going or I'll add you to my detention list,' warned Herbert.

Jit looked at me, mouthed a swear word and then mumbled under his breath, 'Like we care, freak.'

'I BEG YOUR PARDON?'

Herbert's face was all red. Most other kids would have pooped it but Jit just grinned.

'Nuttin', sir,' he said. 'Can you stop talking though – I mean how are we supposed to get to registration if you keep us here in the corridor?'

'Just get going,' Herbert told us through gritted teeth.

'Later,' said Jit, as we walked down towards our form room.

Mrs Dooher was waiting for us as we arrived and I pulled up a chair next to Imtiaz and Hannah, two more of my friends. Jit couldn't find a seat so he stood where he was, like he was lost.

'Grab a seat, Jit,' said Mrs Dooher in her soft Liverpool accent.

'I'm OK standing, miss,' he said.

'You can always sit on my knee,' said Suky, the other friend in our little gang of six.

'Or mine,' added Grace.

'He'd *love* that,' grinned Hannah.

As the class started to giggle, Jit didn't move and

looked to me for help. I budged up and he came across and shared my seat with me.

'We need more chairs, miss!' shouted a lad called Dilip.

'Yes – we do,' agreed Mrs Dooher. 'It's just a shame that so many get broken by you lot.'

'Ain't our fault,' said Dilip's mate, Mohammed.

'It *isn't* our fault, Mohammed,' corrected Mrs Dooher.

'Yeah, but . . .'

Mrs Dooher ignored him.

'Right – there are a lot of notices to get through so listen up, class. And can someone take charge of collecting entries for the school quiz. I need four of you to enter.'

As she spoke, I opened my bag to show Jit the PlayStation games. I sold lots of stuff at school to make a bit of pocket money. It was easy to do. My brother always had things to sell, and often I'd take the money and give Jit some of it. Most of the time he helped to flog the stuff anyway. 'How much?' he whispered.

'Gussie said a tenner but I reckon twelve, man. That way he gets nine quid and we get three quid to share,' I whispered back.

'Nice,' replied Jit.

'Anything you'd like to share with us, Dean?' asked Mrs Dooher.

'Nah, nuttin', miss,' I replied.

'What about five million pounds – you'd love to share that!' shouted Dilip.

'If I had five million pounds why would I want to share it wit' your ugly face?' I asked.

'OK, lads! That's enough. Get to your lessons,' said Miss.

The room filled with the sound of chairs scraping on the floor and the hustle of bags and coats. I winked at Jit and told him we'd go over the stuff at break.

'Go over what?' asked Grace.

'Mind your own, Sister Gee,' I told her.

'You talking about Year Nine girls again?' asked Hannah.

'That's disgusting,' said Suky.

'Stinky bums,' added Grace, jokingly.

I didn't say anything straight away. Instead I counted to ten, waiting for Imtiaz to say something that he thought was mature. Something to back up Suky. I got to three.

'. . . yeah – that's terrible,' he said, looking at the girls.

'Like you don't eye up fit women,' said Jit, wading in on my side as usual.

'I don't do things like that,' replied Imtiaz, acting all big and clever.

'What about that time when we went into town for your birthday – you remember . . .?' I turned to the girls. 'He showed us this proper babe that worked in Debenhams—'

'Shut up, Dean,' said Imtiaz, quickly.

'We don't want to know anyway,' Hannah told us both.

'Don't worry – it's not your fault,' Suky said to me. 'Your hormones will catch up in a couple of years.'

'Nice one!' grinned Hannah.

I looked at Jit and then the rest of them. 'Come on,' I said to Jit, pretending to be hurt. 'We know when we ain't welcome.'

Jit was about to say something but I grabbed him by the arm and pulled him out of the room.

'But what's in the bag?' Grace called out behind us.

'Not telling you! You called us *stinky bums*,' I shouted back.

'Stinky bum!' I heard her reply as me and Jit joined the surge of kids heading for the first lesson. It was like falling into a fast flowing river.

At break, we went and hid in one of the cubicles in the toilets and locked the door. I opened my bag and got out a handful of games. Jit looked through them.

'It's mostly old stuff,' he said, not impressed.

'Yeah, but that's what they's all playing,' I reminded him.

'Ain't you got no new releases or anything?'

I shook my head at him as I heard someone come into the toilets, and lowered my voice.

'It's about making dough, bruv. We can shift these easy.'

'Yeah but . . .'

Someone approached the cubicle and I put a finger to my lips. As I waited for the person to go away, I saw some graffiti on the wall. Someone had tried to wipe it away but hadn't finished the job and I could still make out the words to a rap that I had written about Herbert. I smiled at Jit and pointed at the wall. Jit shrugged. Whoever was listening walked out and we opened the door.

'I'll start asking around,' said Jit.

'Yeah – twelve quid each, remember.'

'Cheaper than Asda,' replied Jit, walking out of the toilets. I followed him.

Out in the corridor I spotted a lad called Jason Patel. He was a bully and he hated me and Jit. I tried not to catch his eye but didn't manage it.

'What you lookin' at?' he asked, as the two lads he was with started to grin.

'Nuttin',' I told him, going to walk off.

Jason grabbed my arm and squeezed it.

'Best not be either!' he warned. 'Look at me like that again and I'll kick your head in.'

From nowhere Jit appeared and shoved Jason in the chest. 'Move!' he shouted.

Everyone in the corridor stopped to stare. I looked at Jit and hoped he would get the look on my face and leave it alone. But Jit gets a bit funny about stuff and I could tell that he was in one of his moods.

'You stupid?' asked Jason.

'Leave him alone,' said Jit.

Jason let go of my arm and squared up to Jit. He was at least five inches taller than my mate and he was hard as nails. Everyone in school avoided him if they could. Not Jit though. Just as I was about to calm the whole thing down and say sorry, Jason slapped Jit and then head-butted him. I felt my whole body go tense and my stomach fell. Jit just stood there though, his eyes watering. There was blood around his nose.

'You want some more?' asked Jason, standing back, holding his hands in fists.

'If you like,' replied Jit, in a whisper.

'You're mad, mate,' grinned Jason. 'You must like gettin' beat up.'

Jit looked at Jason. His eyes were wild.

'My mum hits me harder than that,' he told Jason.

Jason grabbed his hair and punched him a few more times. I jumped in and tried to stop it but Jason's friends pushed me out of the way. When Jason let Jit go there was blood all down his top and he was crying.

'You don't ever leave it, do you?' spat Jason, before walking off quickly with his mates, disappearing outside just as Mr Singh, our football coach, arrived with Miss Khan, who taught English.

'What's happened here?' asked Singh.

Someone shouted that Jit had been beaten up.

'Is that what happened, Jit?' asked Singh.

Jit wiped his eyes but didn't say a word.

'Who saw Jit getting beaten up?' Miss Khan asked the crowd, only no one replied because they were too scared of Jason Patel to snitch on him.

I began to say something but Jit glared at me and I shut up.

'It was nuttin', sir,' he told Singh. 'I bumped into the door.'

Singh looked at Jit and shook his head.

'Come on,' he said to him. 'Let's get you to the medical room.'

I started to follow but Singh told me to stay where I was.

'I think I need to have a little chat with Jit on my own,' he said to me.

I shrugged and watched Jit being led away, as Grace and Hannah walked up, looking all worried.

'What happened?' asked Hannah.

I shrugged again.

'I dunno – we was just walking out of the loo and Jason grabbed me and that. Then he beat up Jit.'

Grace's face fell and tears welled up in her eyes.

'Is he all right?' she asked.

'Dunno – Singhy took him to the medical room,' I replied.

'Did he grass on Jason?' asked Hannah.

'Nah – he'll just get beat up again if he does.'

Grace told us that she was going to see if Jit was OK and Hannah said that someone should stitch Jason up. But that wasn't going to happen and Hannah knew it too. I picked up my bag and walked off to our next lesson, still in shock at what had happened. It was out of nothing too, like being hit by lightning or something. But our school is like that sometimes.

THREE

I didn't see Jit again for the rest of the day and when I went round to his house in the evening, the curtains were drawn. No one answered the door when I knocked so I went home and played music all night. Gussie came into my room around half past ten and asked me if I'd made any money. I told him that I was going to get on with it the following day.

'Seen yer mate, Jit, earlier,' he said.

'Where?' I asked.

'Down Evington Road – with his face all mash-up. He hit a parked bus or summat?'

'Nah – just some fight he got into at school.'

I played with the idea of telling Gussie all about Jason Patel and his bullying, but in the end I didn't say anything. Gussie would have sorted Jason out too, but then the whole school would know that I was scared of Jason and called in my older brother to fight for me.

That was a rep I could do without. Instead I listened to tunes until I fell asleep.

The next morning I called for Jit as usual but got no reply. All the curtains were drawn and I couldn't hear a sound. I waited for about five minutes and knocked as hard as I could but it didn't help. I decided that Jit was taking the day off and walked to Grace's house. But when I got to the bus stop Grace didn't turn up either, and I had to ride to school with Robert and Wesley sitting behind me, talking about the latest chapter of that book. The one that I thought they had made up. I didn't get involved this time though. Instead, I started making up a rhyme in my head about Jit. I didn't get very far before I got bored and in the end I just sat and watched the world go by until it was time to get off.

As I got into my form room though, Jit was already there, laughing about something with Grace. His face was swollen round one eye and his nose was twice its normal size. I walked over and pulled up a chair by Hannah, who Jit and me had known since we were little.

'Hey, Dean,' she said, smiling like she was mad.

'Sister Aitch.'

'You look lost. What's up?'

I shrugged.

'Nuttin',' I replied.

'Must be something because your face looks like it's been slapped hard by a big man with rings on,' she told me.

'I just been on a wild goose chase – that's all. First I called for Jit and then I waited for Sister Gee but they didn't show. And then I get to school and here they are . . . *early*.'

'Yeah, I thought that was a bit weird. They were here before me and that's *never* happened before.'

Jit looked over at me just then and I nodded to him, all cool and that. He raised an eyebrow and then got out of his seat and walked over.

'Yes, D!' he said smiling.

'Easy.'

'Whassup, man?'

'Where was you this mornin'? I called for you and then I walked down to the stop,' I told him.

'Yeah – sorry 'bout that. I went round to Grace's house early and we got a lift in from her dad . . .' he replied, watching my face.

'What – and you never even waited for me?'

I realized that I sounded like a whining little kid and I wished that I hadn't opened my mouth.

'I was well early, bro. I couldn't sleep and then I had to just get out of the house – my mum was stressin' me.'

'Oh.'

'She's been playin' up and that . . . and I'm gettin' the flak.' He began to explain, but then something in his eyes changed and he grinned a big wide smile and changed the subject.

'You see that Misha in Year Ten – the one with the green eyes? Rude!' he said.

I laughed. It was his business and he would tell me when he was good and ready. Instead, I let it go and went with him.

'Rude ain't the word, bro,' I said, before singing a little rhyme that I copied from my favourite reggae artist. I was just about to get to the best bit when Mrs Dooher walked in and told me to be quiet.

'But *miss*,' I complained. 'I was about to get to the nasty bit, innit.'

'Save it for the playground,' Mrs Dooher replied, shuffling through a load of papers.

Grace smiled at me.

'What's the next bit?' she said.

'Too dutty fe you, Sister Gee. I don't want no one talkin' 'bout how I corrupted no little innocent gal.'

'I *hate* you,' joked Grace.

'You don't even know what he was on about,' added Hannah.

'*Yeah*,' joined in Jit.

'Anyway, my brother used to play that tune and it's dirty,' continued Hannah. 'Seriously, Grace, you're better off not knowing what comes next.'

'*Oh!* You horrible people!' said Grace, like a three-year-old who didn't get an ice cream.

'Grace!'

'Sorry, miss,' she said, going red.

I whispered to her, 'I'll tell you when you're a woman.'

Grace gave me a strange look and then she stuck her fingers up at me. I stuck my tongue out and then listened as Mrs Dooher told us a load of uninteresting things about school.

At lunch time I sat with my friends in one of the computer rooms and pretended that I was interested in the school magazine. Hannah, Imi and Suky had taken over and they acted like it was theirs. Every now and again I said something to wind them up – like Imi would ask if anyone had any ideas for a future story and I'd suggest the mating rituals of cockroaches or something – but mostly I just let them get on with it. I didn't mind. I spent the time chatting to Jit or thinking up rhymes. But that lunch time I had other things on my mind. Jit was messing about on a computer as I spoke to him. He was getting angry with it.

'Stupid rules!' he said for about the tenth time.

'Leave that, man,' I said to him. 'Let's go and flog some of these games.'

'Supposed to be workin' on the school paper,' he reminded me.

I thought about it for a moment. 'Let's go and do some research then! Out there in the wild corridors of Devana High. Gotta keep in touch with the readers and that . . .' I said.

'The wannabe adults ain't gonna go for that,' said Jit, talking about Suky and Imi.

'Jus' lef dat to me, my brother,' I told him.

I turned in my chair and watched as Imi tried to work out a problem with the software that Grace's dad had donated to the school. It was a design thing, one that helped to create newspaper templates and magazines but it may as well have been a Latin book to me.

'*Yo!* Editor *bwoi* . . . me an' Jit are gonna head out and do some research, man,' I shouted.

Imi looked up from the screen and grinned.

'Research? Into what?' he asked. '*Misha?*'

'Yeah, man,' I grinned back, 'we're gonna write about the difference between boys and girls and that . . . *educational*, bro, you get me?'

'Nah – but then again you talk like an idiot,' said Imi, returning to the screen.

'Kiss my fat ass. *Twice*,' I told him, getting up.

'So can we expect a piece on teenagers and their relationships then?' asked Grace, as Jit joined me.

'That sounds a bit lame to me,' I said. 'You might get a lyrics on summat though.'

'What's a "lyrics", Dean?' asked Grace.

'A rhyme, Sister Gee. You know, if poetry was called *lyrics*, I reckon more of the yout' would go for it,' I told her.

'Like them poetry slams at the community centre?' asked Hannah.

'Yeah – you get me?' I replied.

'*Ehhh!* No thanks,' she said, smiling.

'Dunno what you're *missin'*, Sister Aitch,' I said, jokingly.

'I've seen your bedroom,' grinned Hannah. '*Believe me* – I know . . .'

'Evil woman! You can kiss my *double* fat ass. *Three times*,' I replied, heading out of the door with Jit.

We walked out to the tennis courts and stood by the steps. There were groups of kids hanging around and chatting and I unzipped my bag and pulled out a handful of games.

'Go for the rich kids,' I told Jit.

Our school was a bit of an experiment, or at least that's what my dad once told me. They took half of each year group from round my way, an area which was kind of poor, and half of them from the area where Grace, Imi and Suky lived, which was called posh and where everyone had big houses and lots of money. Thing was, *my* family lived in a big house and we had enough money but that didn't make *us* posh, just because of the area we lived in, which I thought was really funny. Adults are some messed up people, with their prejudices and that. Jit eyed up Robert and Wesley, who were with a bunch of their friends. As we walked over I realized that they were still discussing the same book.

'. . . Princess Wondlebarn has got the ancient Flute of Kings,' Wesley was telling everyone else, as I interrupted him.

'And the great goblin, Ganglefart, is going to eat her,' I said.

They looked at me like I was crazy, as Jit grinned. I showed them my goods.

'PlayStation games, man – all the latest stuff. You wan' it, we got it.'

'I don't think you're supposed to sell things at school,' said Robert.

'Who says that?' asked Jit.

'I'm just sure that it's against the rules,' he added.

I looked at Wesley and shrugged.

'Well, if you're gonna play by the rules you may as well go to the local shops and spend big money on them.'

Wesley looked around his group of friends and then spoke. 'Did you say they'd be cheaper?' he asked.

'Less than half price,' I replied, holding out the games for him. 'I want twelve quid. Not a penny less and not ten pound more like in the shops.'

'But they're all copies,' said Robert, after taking one and studying it like a text book.

'That's right – genuine, first generation, burned by my own two hands, copies,' I admitted.

'But—' began Wesley.

'*Wesley, Wesley, Wesley*,' I said. 'When you're at home downloading stuff from the net without paying – that's the same thing.'

'But you can't do that any more,' Robert told me. 'You have to pay now.'

'Even better . . . I'm offering you brand new games.'

Robert looked through the rest, picked out a fantasy game and smiled.

'Twelve pounds, you say.'

'If I'm lyin' I'm flyin', Roberto,' I told him, copying something that I heard in a film once.

'This is really a rather wicked game,' said Robert.

'That's my boy,' I said with a huge grin. 'What's twelve quid when you've got a rather wicked game, right there in your hand?'

Robert looked around his friends, as though he was waiting for one of them to tell him no. When they didn't speak, he pulled out his wallet and handed me the money.

'See? Nuttin' so nice as handin' over yer money when you know that you've got yourself a proper, *one hundred percent* bargain, blood,' I said, as his friends asked to look at the rest of the stash.

'An' remember,' I continued. 'I ain't no supermarket. *Sold as seen*, my likkle fantasy-reading bredren . . . you get me?'

Robert gave me a funny look and shrugged.

FOUR

I asked Jit about Jason on the way home. We were walking up Evington Road, past a load of takeaway shops and my stomach was rumbling as the smell of food wafted around the street.

'I ain't gonna do nuttin',' Jit told me. 'What *can* I do?'

'You didn't have to get involved,' I told him.

'What? And leave my best mate to get picked on – I'd rather get beaten up,' replied Jit.

I was going to say something, but the way Jit had said what he did made me feel proud to have him as my friend. I told him that I would talk to Gussie for him.

'Straighten it out. If you like . . .' I said to him.

Jit shrugged. 'Ain't worth it. If Gussie batters Jason then we'll just get more grief from him. Best just leave it. He'll get his, bro. He's not gonna be bigger than us for the rest of his life, is he?'

'I don't even know why he picks on us,' I said. 'I mean it ain't like we ask for it.'

Jit grinned. 'Apart from the last time, when I shoved him,' he said.

'Yeah well – thanks for that. You saved me there.'

We crossed a side street and walked past a grocer's. There was an old man, a local homeless bloke, standing outside the shop. He had grey hair that was matted into dirty dreadlocks and he stank. As the people entering and leaving the shop tried to ignore him, he held out a wooden stick like it was a sword and pretended to fight someone.

'Mash yuh up!' he was shouting at no one.

We walked past quickly so that he wouldn't try to talk to us like he normally did. We called him MC Nutty, although I had no idea what his real name was.

'How much we make on the games?' Jit asked me.

'Give me a moment and I'll do you a profit and loss sheet,' I said.

I stopped and opened my bag, counting my stash. There had been thirty in there in the morning and now there were nineteen. Not bad for one day.

'We sold eleven – that's over a hundred quid,' I told him.

Jit's eyes nearly popped out of his head.

'That's some good dough,' he said.

'Still gotta give Gussie his money out of that,' I reminded him.

'So what's that make then?' he asked.

'Three quid a game – work it out.'

We walked on, both of us quiet as our brains tried to do the maths. It was like a contest to see who would come up with the figures first and I was confident that I'd win. Too confident though.

'One hundred and thirty-two total,' I said. 'So about forty quid for us.'

'Nah,' said Jit, correcting me. 'It's ninety-nine for Gussie and thirty-three for us.'

I looked at him in amazement. Jit hated maths and never paid attention in school. Maybe I'd found another way to teach him, I thought, as I dreamed up my own teach yourself maths text book, one that would make me loads of money.

'. . . So that's sixteen-fifty each,' he concluded.

'Yeah – I'll double-check it at home but I think you're right,' I said.

Jit stopped at the end of his street and looked at me.

'Any chance you can let me have a fiver?' he asked.

'Yeah – later. I'll bring it round,' I replied, not getting what he meant.

'I meant now, bro,' he said, looking embarrassed.

'Oh – right . . . yeah, no worries,' I said.

Jit waited for a moment before explaining. 'It's just that my mum is workin' late and she ain't left me no dinner,' he said.

'That's cool, bro. You don't have to explain,' I told him.

'So I need some dough to get some chips or summat,' he continued. 'And I ain't got no bus fare for the mornin'.'

And then he just stopped, like he'd realized what he'd said and didn't like it. I pulled out some money and gave it to him. It was a tenner.

'There you go, brother,' I said. 'Although you could always eat round at mine . . . Mum would love it. She's always complaining that I don't bring me mates home.'

'Maybe another night,' said Jit, pocketing the money. 'I'll check you tomorrow.'

'I was gonna bring the rest round later,' I said to him.

'I gotta do some stuff for me mum,' said Jit, as he turned to leave.

I was going to say something but I left it and watched him walk off up the street. I knew something was up with him, but I didn't want to be all girlie and ask him about it. I knew that he'd tell me soon enough. Instead I headed home and wondered whether I should have charged fifteen pounds for the games instead.

Gussie was waiting when I got in and asked for his money before I'd had a chance to sit down.

'Hol' yer horses, bro, I ain't even got me jacket off yet,' I protested.

'Just hand me my money, Dean, and stop with yer nonsense.'

'Let me sort out my stuff first,' I said, not wanting Gussie to see that I had more money than I was supposed to have.

I took off my jacket and headed up two flights of stairs to my room, locking the door when I got in. I counted out the money quickly, hiding the rest of mine and Jit's, and then I took Gussie's cut downstairs.

'Cool,' he said, as he counted it. 'Them things goin' like hot cakes.'

'Yeah,' I agreed. 'Should get rid of the rest by the end of the week. You gettin' any more?'

'Yeah, man – as many as you need. Got something even better for you soon,' he told me.

I looked at him and raised an eyebrow.

'What?' I asked.

'Mobiles, bro. Nuff of dem . . .'

I found the remote for the telly and turned it on, sitting down but ignoring the screen. 'How much?' I asked him.

'Dunno yet,' Gussie told me. 'My mate, Raj, is getting them. Top of the range too.'

'Raj owns that phone shop on East Park Road don't he?'

'*Yeah* – so what?' asked my brother.

'So why can't he sell them there?' I said to him.

It made perfect sense to me. What was the point in having the shop if you gave other people phones to sell?

'Extra stock – off the books and that, you get me?' Gussie said. 'My man needs to get rid so I'm buying the excess.'

'Still don't get it,' I admitted.

'All *you* need to get is the dough for the phones. You'll make a *load* on them,' promised Gussie.

I was about to say something else but I stopped

when I realized that he was right. I wouldn't be making small change out of them. But then again, I thought, would anyone at school have the money to buy phones in the first place? Gussie stood up and told me he was off to see a mate.

'You comin' back for dinner?'

'Nah – tell mum I'll get summat in town,' he said. 'I gotta do a shift with Dad at eight, anyways.'

'Good,' I said. 'Means more food for me, Mr Rotund.'

'You what?' he said, looking puzzled.

'Nuttin', bro. Get a dictionary,' I replied.

'What – and end up like you? No thanks.'

He walked out and left me to think about who I'd try to sell the mobiles to. My gramps walked in as I was thinking and farted real loud. It sounded like he had thunder in his pants and the smell was like something that had died.

'*Gramps!*' I said, laughing. 'Tha's nasty, man.'

'A nuh nuttin'. Betta fe get it out than keep it in,' he replied, sitting down to watch the telly with me. Not even a second thought to the nuclear fart he had just ripped – nasty!

* * *

After my dinner, I walked to Grace's house. She had called to say that her and Hannah were in her basement, going over stuff for the school paper. I said that I'd come over, but when she asked me to call for Jit I told her that he was busy.

'Oh right,' she'd replied, sounding disappointed.

'What – I'm not good enough on my own?' I teased.

'Yeah!' she said quickly. 'I just hoped that Jit would come round too.'

'You'll have to forget about snogging him for one night,' I told her.

'Stinky git,' she said.

When I got to her house, her mum let me in and asked me how I was.

'Haven't seen you for a few days,' she said.

'I've been busy, Mrs Parkhurst,' I said, in my best accent, trying to impress.

'Homework?' she asked, smiling at me.

'Yes – and other stuff, er . . . things,' I replied.

'Well I'd better let you get downstairs what with the deadline for the paper looming.'

'OK.'

I headed down the stairs, hearing a White Stripes song playing.

'Elvis is in da building!' I said as I walked in.

'Greetings, Elvis – tell me, does Heaven have reality TV?' asked Hannah.

'Eh?'

'Reality TV,' she repeated.

'What about it, you loony tunes?' I said.

''Cos if it does, do the losers have to go to hell?'

I just looked at her and shook my head. 'You need to get out more, Sister Aitch. Thirteen and with a head full of nonsense already . . .'

'Oh *hello*, Grace – thanks for inviting me *round* – think I'll *ignore* you though and pretend like you're not even here!' said Grace.

'Easy, Sister Gee – didn't see you there,' I joked.

'There'll be trouble, my lad,' she said, imitating Mr Black.

'Oh, be firm with me,' I begged. 'Firm but fair!'

'Will you both shut up,' said Hannah.

I stuck my tongue out at her and went and racked up the balls on Grace's pool table, ready to play a game.

'Who's first for a beatin'?' I said.

'We asked you round to help with the paper,' said Grace.

'What's wrong with Imi and Suky?' I asked. 'They're the *editors*.'

'Imi's at some family do and Suky has got some homework to do,' replied Hannah.

'So you sent for the substitute?' I asked.

'No – you're supposed to be helping us too,' said Grace.

Hannah shook her head and walked over to me, grabbing the pool cue from my hand.

'From what I remember, Dean, it's your fault that we have to do this anyway,' she said, menacingly.

'Easy, sister . . . no need to get violent,' I said with a grin.

Hannah poked me in the chest and then cracked into a smile.

'I tell you what – it's only 'cos I've known you since we were three that I don't stick this cue where the sun don't shine!'

'Anyone like a drink?' Grace's dad interrupted from the foot of the stairs.

Hannah went bright red.

'Can I have a juice please, Dad,' said Grace.

'Yeah, me too,' I said. 'Please.'

'And what about you, Hannah? Once you've

finished putting that cue where the sun doesn't shine,' grinned Mr Parkhurst.

'Can I have a coffee?' asked Hannah, grinning back.

Grace's dad suddenly got all excited.

'Ah coffee! Good choice, Hannah, only I've just this morning acquired—' he began.

'You're in for it now,' said Grace. 'He got a new toy this morning – a coffee machine – and now he's going to bore us all silly with how it works and we'll never get this work done.'

I thought about the coffee machine at my dad's bar. 'Has it got one of them steamy thingys?' I asked.

'Sure has,' said Mr Parkhurst.

'Cool!' said Hannah.

'I'll show you how it works if you like,' said Mr Parkhurst.

Grace let out a moan and then started calling everything she could see, the pens, the paper, the pool table, *everything*, stinky bums.

FIVE

Soon everyone in our year knew about the PlayStation games and Jit and me managed to shift the lot in two days. I even got a few more off Gussie on demand – they were going faster than bullets. By the Thursday evening of that week, we were sitting in the computer room, counting our money and waiting to play football for Devana High in a school league match. It was against our most hated rivals, a school from the other side of the city, and we were really up for it. The last time we had played against them, it had been at their school and we'd been racially abused throughout the game by their supporters. Now it was our turn to get some revenge. Imi, who captained the team, kept on giving us little pep talks to get us going and even Mr Singh was excited. The whole year knew about it and loads of supporters were going to watch the game.

'Can't wait,' said Jit, pocketing his money after counting it again.

'This time we're gonna stuff 'em,' I said, remembering how they had won a penalty in the final minute of the last game.

'Yeah – this time the ref's gonna be our coach.'

Mr Singh would be running the match, just as the other team's coach did at their place, so they wouldn't be getting any dodgy decisions. Their coach had been useless – ignoring all the abuse and telling us to get on with the game, like it was OK to get called those names. I'd had to bite my lip throughout the game, something that I don't like doing but when Mr Singh had lodged an official complaint, nothing was done about it. It was pure Babylon, as my dad had said, when I told him.

'They ain't gonna chat no rubbish either,' I said. 'Not with our fans there.' I turned to the girls. 'You lot comin' to watch us later?' I asked.

'*Yeah!*' replied Grace and Hannah together.

'Cool,' I said, waiting for the cheeky remark. It was Grace who made it.

'We couldn't *possibly* miss the opportunity to watch you three in your *little* shorts.'

'All that lovely man muscle . . .' added Hannah.

'More like *boy* muscle,' corrected Grace.

'Like twiglets with bottoms attached to them, even.'

I shook my head at them. 'Girls, girls . . . what you gonna *do*? You is *too* embarrassed to admit that we is *fine*, so you mek joke to cover it up . . . it's *sad*.'

'You saying I've got skinny legs?' asked Jit, suddenly waking up to the conversation.

'Er . . . *yeah*. Have you looked in a *mirror* recently?' said Hannah.

Jit looked at me.

'Don't be askin' me, bro – I don't never look 'pon your legs no-how,' I said.

'A good thing too,' said Jit.

'I think you've got *nice* legs, Jit,' said Grace.

Jit looked at me again and I shrugged.

'Er . . . yeah . . . look we gonna do this paper or what?' he said, changing the subject.

Hannah winked at Grace then grinned at me. 'See how the bwoi a change subject,' she teased.

'Shut up, Hannah,' said Jit, glaring at her.

'It's OK if you fancy Grace – you only have to say so.'

'Oh get lost!' replied Jit.

I could see that he was getting wound up so I gave Grace a nudge and she jumped in.

'Leave Jit alone, Hannah-Banana,' she said.

'I was only playin',' replied Hannah.

'I *suggest*,' boomed a voice from the door, 'that you *play* a little less and *work* a little more.'

We turned to see Mr Black and Mrs Lee-Cross, our Maths teacher, at the door.

'Sorry, sir,' said Grace. 'We're just getting it done now.'

'Good, good,' said Black.

'Anything interesting in it?' asked Lee-Cross.

'No fractions – if that's what you mean,' replied Jit.

Mrs Lee-Cross smiled. 'I could set you some if you like,' she answered.

'We're only short of one feature,' said Hannah quickly, before Jit got himself into trouble with his big mouth.

'So are we missing the deadline?' asked Black. 'Only I've told everyone that it will be ready next week and I can't be made to look silly.'

'Oh, no, sir,' said Grace. 'We'll get something in.'

'What about a bit of poetry?' asked Black.

'What a splendid idea,' beamed Lee-Cross.

The others looked at me.

'Er . . . could it be like modern stuff?' I asked.

'Well I've been re-reading William Blake recently so I was hoping for something traditional – maybe a piece on Blake's life and a few of his poems?' said Mr Black.

'Oh,' I said, trying not to sound disappointed but failing.

'What do you have in mind, Mr Chambers?' asked Black.

'Well I was gonna write something that was about the school – and maybe write about how rap is like modern poetry.'

'Rap?' began Mrs Lee-Cross, frowning.

'Oh yes, Nancy,' said Black, using Lee-Cross's first name by mistake. 'I've been reading a lot of articles recently about youth culture and the rise of urban poetry.'

Mrs Lee-Cross went slightly red and looked away but Black didn't even notice.

'Maybe we could cover the poetry slam at the community centre near us,' added Hannah. 'There's one on Saturday.'

'Splendid idea!' he boomed. 'You can cover that,

and Dean, I'd like you to do an original piece too, in the *urban* style.'

'OK,' I agreed.

'Now get on with it and mind you're good and fit for this evening, lads – I've a steak dinner riding on you lot winning,' he grinned.

With that he marched out of the room and Lee-Cross followed.

'He's nuts,' said Hannah.

'Proper loopy,' agreed Jit.

'Well at least he's not a complete ogre,' said Grace, defending him.

'Yeah,' I agreed, despite myself. 'How many head teachers you reckon there are that know about rap and want it in *their* school paper?'

Jit looked at me like I was nuts.

'Poetry's boring,' said Hannah.

'No it ain't,' I argued. 'Not really – we just get taught old stuff, that's all.'

'*Boring*,' yawned Jit, agreeing with Hannah.

'What about Eminem?'

'He's a *rapper*,' said Hannah.

'I read something that called him an urban poet,' Grace told us.

'*Exactly*,' I replied. 'All them rappers is like poets – they just ain't called poets because they swear and that.'

'You're wrong in the head, bro,' said Jit.

'So you're saying poetry can be *fun*?' asked Hannah.

'Yeah,' I said, looking at Grace, who winked at me.

'Prove it,' challenged Hannah.

'OK then,' I replied. 'I'm gonna write a lyric about school for the paper.'

'Can't wait,' said Jit, sarcastically.

'Better get on with it,' Hannah told me. 'We need it by the end of the week.'

Jason Patel caught up with me as I was walking to my next lesson. He was on his own and as I walked by, trying to ignore him, he grabbed me by the arm.

'I hear you've got games to sell,' he said.

'*Did* have,' I replied.

'So why didn't you come to me?' he asked.

I shrugged.

'You got any more?' he said, loosening his grip. I pulled my arm away.

'Nah – sold out.'

He moved his head closer to my face.

'Next time you got stuff to sell, you let me see first, yeah?'

'Yeah, cool.'

'I mean it. I find out that you're selling stuff and don't tell me, I'm not gonna be happy.'

'OK,' I said, turning to walk away.

'Best remember, too,' he threatened.

I walked into my lesson and sat down next to Grace. There must have been something in my face because she asked me if I was OK. The lesson was just about to start and Mr Woods told us all to shut up, so I whispered my reply.

'I'm fine. Just bumped into a snake in the corridor, that's all.'

The rest of the afternoon dragged and by the time school finished I had forgotten about what Jason had said. I was too wound up about the football. I ran down to the changing rooms with Jit and we started talking about the game, and how many goals we were going to score. Imtiaz was waiting for us, already half changed and we started to get ready too. The rest of the team started arriving soon afterwards, and as I sat on the wooden bench, with my boots next to me, I watched Mr Singh bring in a net bag, full of footballs.

'On me head, Singhy!' I shouted.

Mr Singh grinned at me.

'The other school are going to be about half an hour yet so I want you to get out there and get warmed up. Remember I want the stretches done properly *before* you start kicking the balls around.'

'Yeah, yeah,' I said. 'Just pass me a football, sir.'

Mr Singh took a ball out of the net and threw it to me. I grabbed hold of it in one hand, picked up my boots with the other, and headed outside, with Jit and Imtiaz following.

SIX

Half of our year had turned out to support us when we got to the pitch. I looked around for the girls and saw them standing by the halfway line. I walked over, booting the ball up into the air and then chasing after it. It bounced around the centre circle and I misjudged, running straight underneath it. Jit controlled it behind me and started to do keep-ups, which he was really good at. Then he passed the ball to Imi who trapped it, and pushed it on to me with his other foot. We did this for a few minutes and then started doing stretches. As I bent forward to touch my toes, I heard a wolf-whistle from behind me. I straightened up and turned to see Hannah grinning.

'Nice bum!' she shouted, before bursting into giggles with Suky and Grace. I stuck two fingers up at them and went back to my warm up.

One by one, the rest of the team started to turn up

on the pitch. They started their warm up routines but I'd already finished mine, so I got the ball and kicked it towards one of the goals. It ran along the ground into the net and got stuck. I jogged over and pulled it free, turning to see Jit and Imi by the penalty spot.

'You go in goal for a minute,' said Imi, as I threw the ball to him. He placed it on the penalty spot and took five steps backwards. Then he ran slowly to the ball and sent it flying past my head, back into the net.

'YEAH!!!' came a shout from the sidelines, as Suky and Hannah jumped up and down.

I threw the ball to Jit next and looked for Grace. She was standing with Robert and Wesley, who must have been forced to come along because they never watched football. Robert's face was so red that I could see it from where I stood and I watched as Grace flirted with them both, giggling and playing with her hair. I wondered what she was up to as the ball sailed over my head again.

'GOAAAAL!!!' I heard Jit shout as he did a little jig, copying a Manchester United player, his arms out at his side.

'Only goal you're gonna get,' I said to him. 'You don't ever score in the real games.'

'I'm the creator,' he said. 'Weren't for me you'd never get the ball 'cos you don't like tackling.'

'What you on about? I'm like Mr T for Tackle.'

'More like Little Miss Tackle,' said Imi.

'Leave it, posh boy,' I told him. 'You stick to yer books and yer computer. Dis here's a ghetto bwoi game.'

'Shut up, Dean,' said Imi.

'See? You know I'm right.'

I walked away from the goal and took the ball with me, placing it just outside the penalty box, about twenty yards from the goal. Simon, our goalkeeper, jogged to the goal line and turned to face me, as some of the girls in the crowd started to sing 'Devana, Devana!'

'Top corner, Deano,' said Simon, waiting for me to take my shot.

I concentrated on where I was going to put the ball, and then tried to curl it past the keeper. But I caught the ball wrong and it skidded across the ground into Simon's hands.

'RUBBISH!' shouted someone from the crowd, as I swore at myself.

Mr Singh blew his whistle and gathered us all together in the centre circle.

'The other team are five minutes away,' he said, 'so you've got fifteen minutes to kill, at least.'

He looked at me and grinned before speaking.

'I suggest that *some* of you use that time to practise your shooting skills,' he said.

Jit and Imi started laughing at me but I ignored them and went over to where the girls were standing.

'Deano! Deano!' sang Hannah, before wolf-whistling again.

'Yes, yes, sisters!' I said, holding my arms out and my palms upwards, like a real poser.

'Nice shorts,' said Suky.

'Must feel real good to know you got a man like me standing talking to you,' I joked.

'Oooh yeah,' said Hannah. 'I'm gonna fall over with excitement in a minute.'

'See me?' I boasted. 'I am the don, the don, the king champion!'

Suky and Hannah burst into laughter.

'See how your head gets bigger every day,' said Suky.

'Hush up and go kiss yer boyfriend,' I told her.

'Who's my boyfriend?' she asked.

'Imi – don't tell me you ain't checking him, Suky. I *know* . . .'

Suky looked at Hannah.

'*See?*' she said. 'Boys don't know anything . . .'

Grace walked up to us and smiled.

'Hey, Brother Dee,' she said, copying my joke.

I was about to pull her up, but Hannah suddenly whispered to us. 'Miss Khan's here,' she said, like that was supposed to be a big time secret or something.

'And?' I asked.

'*Miss Khan? Mr Singh?*' whispered Suky.

'God – don't you know *anything*?' added Grace.

'They're going out with each other,' said Hannah, like the walking gossip magazine that she is.

'How you know that?' I asked.

'It's like, *sooo* obvious,' said Suky, in an American accent.

'You lot are like a bunch of cackling hags,' I said. 'All you do is chat.'

'It's true,' said Grace. 'I saw them together in town . . . they were *holding hands*.'

'Big deal, man.'

The girls looked at each other and shook their heads in disgust.

'You just run along back to your little game,' said Hannah.

'*Boys*,' added Suky.

'Blabber mout' witches,' I said with a smile, before returning to the other lads.

In our first year at Devana High, Mr Black had managed to get floodlights for our main pitch. It was used for games all year round, and by the local community too. So, by the time the other school arrived, the lights were just coming on, even though it was still daylight. I watched the opposition walk onto the pitch as our supporters booed them and called them names. Not racist ones, like their fans had done to us, just funny ones. The players didn't look around them, they walked on with their heads down, like they were worried. I pointed it out to Imi, who just grinned.

'Let's give them a good reason to be worried,' he said, looking at Jit, who was known for making really hard tackles in the first few minutes of every game, just to see how the other teams reacted.

'I'm ready,' said Jit.

Mr Singh had a quick word with their teacher, who was going to be a linesman, and then signalled to Mr Wilson, who was watching the opposite line. He called Imi and their captain to the centre, spoke to them and then put the ball on the centre spot. They kicked off and passed the ball all the way back to their keeper. I pushed ahead, taking up my position as a forward, coming face to face with one of the biggest players, a lad called Johnno. 'You're getting stuffed this time,' I said to him, watching the ball as it sailed over my head, towards our goal.

'You wish,' said Johnno, running to the halfway line with me.

Jit got hold of the ball in midfield and sent it skidding along the ground to the right, where one of our players, Gary, controlled it, before skipping past their left back and running in towards their goal. Their centre half got in quickly though and made a tackle, winning the ball and sending it back into the middle where I challenged for it with Johnno. He used his elbows to beat me to it and sent me sprawling to the ground, as he headed it away. I got up quickly and glared at him.

'Summat wrong, you monkey?' he said quietly.

'You what?'

'You 'eard me,' he said, chasing after the ball again.

I ran with him, fuming, watched him collect it and then slid in, taking the ball and his legs together. He cried out and swore as Mr Singh blew for a free kick.

'Leave it out, Dean,' Singhy said to me.

'He was callin' me racist names again,' I told him.

Mr Singh looked at me and nodded.

'Well if I hear him – he's going off. You leave the punishment to me,' he said.

The trouble was that Johnno and his team-mates were being clever about it. As the game turned into a scrappy mess, they taunted us in whispers, so that Singhy couldn't hear them, and one by one, we got angrier and angrier, even the white lads in our team, who hated the racism as much as we did. Near the end of the first half, I was running around like an angry bull. I had one chance which I put over the bar and another that I missed wide, and with about five minutes left I heard Johnno taunting me again.

'This is an English game,' he said. 'You darkies ain't no good at it.'

Jit jogged up beside me as Johnno walked away, laughing to his team-mates.

'What did he say?' Jit asked.

'Usual stuff,' I replied.

'I'm getting vex!' Jit told me.

'Leave it,' I said. 'Let's just beat 'em with the ball.'

But Jit, as usual, didn't listen. Gary, Imi and another lad, Matt, created a good opening which their keeper sent out for a corner, and we waited in the box for the delivery. As I was running around, trying to find a space, someone tripped me up and then I heard someone whisper in my face.

'Ever see a flyin' gorilla? Watch the replay.'

I looked up and saw a boot connect with my abuser's face. Shouting went up and the two teams got into a scuffle, pushing and shouting and swearing. Gary had Johnno in a headlock and was punching his head and Jit was laying into the lad that had tripped me up. It was like a war zone. When it was all over, Johnno, Gary and Jit were sent off and a few yellow cards were shown to some of the others. I went mad at half time, calling Mr Singh a coward. But he ignored me and said that he wasn't going to tolerate fighting, regardless of the reasons behind it.

The second half went by without any more incidents and right at the end Imi scored from a free kick to win the game but no one was cheering or clapping. Gary and Jit had told everyone watching what had happened and as the opposing team left the pitch some of our fans started to boo them. Then someone threw a drink over their coach and someone else threw a punch, as the crowd surrounded them, mostly the lads but some of the girls too. Mr Singh ran in to try and calm it down, pushing people away, but the atmosphere was ugly, like they say in the news, and eventually Mr Black and a few more teachers sorted it all out. Black was going mad, his face all red.

'I'm ashamed of you all!' he was shouting, pushing kids out of the way, yelling at them to go home . . .

SEVEN

'There is a deep sense of shame nestling in my breast this morning, one that I can only attribute to the actions of a small minority of your year, *actions* which took place last night . . .'

The entire year was sitting in the main hall the following morning, listening to Mr Black as he talked about the football. I was right in the middle, sitting next to Hannah and Grace, hoping that he wouldn't pick on Jit or Gary for being sent off. They were both at the back of the hall, Gary with his class, and Jit sitting on his own because he had come in late. When I'd called for him no one answered and he wasn't waiting with Grace when I got to hers either. I don't know where he'd been but I knew it was because he was angry about the game. At least that's what I thought was up with him. Mr Black cleared his throat and continued.

'. . . I'm not *saying* that racism is to be tolerated. It *should* be punished. But not like yesterday. Attacking another school's pupils, *regardless* of what they've done, when they've been invited as *our* guests, is *not* the way of Devana High. It is *not* the civilized response. Now, I know some of you will argue that you were abused and I know that is *wrong*, but it is up to *us*, as your *teachers*, to sort these problems out. You *don't* do it by jostling and jeering a group of pupils and teachers from another school as though they were elks and you were a pack of wolves . . . oh, some of you *may* snigger but that's what *I* saw last night. Bullying, cowardly actions which I *will not* tolerate. Do I make myself *clear*?'

'Yes, sir,' replied about half of our year group.

'Right, now get to lessons, whilst I try and salvage what is left of the goodwill towards our school by telephoning their principal and apologizing in person. Good morning, Year Nine.'

And with that he stormed out of the hall, closely followed by Herbert and Singh. We had English with Herbert and I walked towards the classroom slowly. Jit was waiting outside the hall for me, and he looked like he had slept in his clothes. There was a strange smell coming from him and his hair was a mess.

'You look like you've been dragged through a hedge, backwards,' I said to him.

He looked into my eyes and then down at his feet.

'I couldn't sleep,' he told me. 'I was angry about gettin' sent off and then when I did fall asleep, I couldn't get up and I didn't want to be late for school . . .'

'That's a first,' I told him, smiling.

'Didn't even have time to shower,' he said.

'Yeah, I can smell that for myself,' I joked, but then wished that I hadn't opened my big mouth. Jit looked away.

'Only kiddin', bro,' I said, trying to make up for it.

'You got any more of them games to sell?' he asked me, changing the subject.

'Nah – Gussie's gonna get some more this weekend – should have some next week.'

'Good,' replied Jit. 'I could use the money . . .'

I was going to say something but Jit saw Grace and Hannah coming towards us and got all funny.

'I'm goin' to the toilets to sort out my hair,' he said.

'Never bothered you before,' I said.

'See you in class,' he replied, running off before Hannah and Grace reached us.

They watched him go and shook their heads.

'Strange boy,' said Grace.

'Easy, Grace – don't upset the football hooligans – they might attack us like wolves goin' after elks,' joked Hannah.

'Yeah – what the hell was Black on about?' I asked, not giving Jit another thought.

'Dunno – he's a funny old git,' laughed Hannah.

'Bit harsh on us though,' I said.

'I thought that,' said Grace. 'I mean the other team were being racist – so why should we have to apologize?'

'Exactly,' I told them. 'Seems to me like it's different rules for them schools, you get me?'

'No there aren't,' said Hannah.

'So you explain it then.'

Hannah looked at me and grinned. 'OK – I *will* then . . . er . . . *later* . . . when I've asked me mum,' she said.

When I got home that evening I spent an hour sitting in front of the telly, not really paying attention to what I was watching. Ruby turned up around half-past five with a load of shopping bags and slumped down on the sofa next to me.

'*More* clothes?' I asked.

'None of your business,' she told me.

'How many do you need?'

She looked at me like I was an insect.

'I *change* my clothes – *every* day – not like you, you *dutty* tramp.'

I was about to answer back when my Gramps walked in and sat down too.

'I see yuh a buy more clothes,' he said to Ruby, who groaned.

'Leave it out, Gramps – he's just been saying the same thing. I'm a *girl* – I need to have clothes.'

Gramps shook his head and let out a little sigh. 'Back when I was growin' up in Kingston, me 'ave *one* shirt pon mi back and *one* shoes pon mi foot.'

I grinned at Ruby. It was a story that he always told us.

'So you never had no trousers then?' I asked.

'*Eh?*'

'*Trousers*, Gramps. You walk around in your boxer shorts?'

'You likkle *raas* – of course mi 'ave trouser – two of dem . . . but we never 'ave money like de yout' dem today. You two dunno yuh born, man. Spoil fe true . . .' he replied, shaking his head again.

'Well, we ain't in Jamaica,' said Ruby. 'This is *England* and a girl needs to have clothes.'

Gramps let out a little giggle.

'*Inglan?* Yuh father should 'ave moved yuh *raas* to Jamaica, man. None a dem pickney spoilt like yuh.'

Pickney means 'kids' and Gramps went on to tell us how there was no discipline in English schools which meant that kids had no morals nowadays.

I just kept on grinning at my sister as Gramps went off on one, not stopping to see if we were even listening.

'One cuff pon dem 'ead an' dem soon hush dem mout',' he mumbled.

Gussie walked in just as Gramps was winding up. He told me to come up to his room.

'What for?' I asked, as Gramps turned his attention to the telly and the news.

'Never mind – just get yer skinny backside up the stairs, bro,' replied Gussie.

'Which one of you is helpin' with the dinner tonight?' asked Ruby.

'We'll toss a coin,' said Gussie.

'You best do an' all. I ain't doin' it all on my own

again. You wan' eat, yuh best help wid it,' she warned, sounding just like my mum.

I groaned and followed Gussie up the stairs and into his room, which was at the back of the house. It was a mess, with clothes all over the floor and empty mugs and plates everywhere. There were albums stacked high on a shelf next to a neat little sound system too and on the floor stood two massive speakers that weren't connected up.

'Where'd you get them?' I asked about the speakers.

'Mate,' replied Gussie, as usual. It was like his stock answer to everything.

'So what do you want?' I said, not that I was in any hurry to go back downstairs and peel potatoes or whatever it was that Ruby had lined up for me.

'Phones, my boy,' said Gussie with a grin, putting on a posh accent. 'Mobile communication devices especially for the youths of today. Super, what?'

'Just shut up and let me see them,' I told him.

He picked up a bag from his bed and unzipped it, pulling out a mobile phone. Handing it to me, he threw the bag back down onto the bed. I looked at the black handset. It was a BlackBerry with a camera, Bluetooth and everything.

'Wow – this is cool,' I said, turning it over in my hands. It was so light.

'Them things ain't nothing,' said Gussie. 'There's a new range about to come out, even better . . . Raj is getting me one as soon as they get released.'

'How many you got?' I asked.

'Six – all with the chargers. Should be easy to get rid of,' he said.

'How much?' I asked.

Gussie shrugged. 'Up to you what you charge for them . . .' he said, looking away.

'Nah – I meant how much do you want?'

He picked up the bag again and tipped out the rest. Then he sat down on his bed and played with one of his rings.

'I got 'em for nothing,' he said. 'I told you – they was extra stock that Raj wanted rid of and he owed me some stuff anyways.'

I frowned at him.

'Something wrong with them?' I asked, getting worried.

'Don't be stupid – why would I take a load of dodgy phones? Ain't exactly good business, is it?'

I thought about it for a minute and realized that he

was right. He wouldn't have taken them if they were messed up. As the thought dawned on me, Gussie told me what he wanted.

'Just give us fifty for 'em,' he said.

'Each?'

'Nah – for the lot, baby brother. And don't say that I never look after you.'

Greed took over and I realized that I would make loads of money on them. I looked at my brother who shrugged again, in a 'take it or leave it' kind of way.

'You got a deal,' I told him, grinning like a fool.

I ran up to my room, got out my stash of savings and counted fifty quid. Then I ran back downstairs to give it to Gussie, half expecting him to have changed his mind or laugh and say that it was all a wind-up. The phones were worth over one hundred pounds each in the shops, which meant that I could sell them for seventy quid no problem. It was the deal of the century, the bargain of the millennium. I was well happy. I handed my money to Gussie and grabbed the phones, just as I heard the door bell ring.

EIGHT

'DEAN! Someone to see you,' shouted Ruby.

I stashed the phones in my room and ran down the stairs wondering who it was. When I got to the front door Jit was standing there. He looked really embarrassed and he had a bag with him.

'Yes, Jit – come into the madhouse,' I said, shutting the door behind him.

'Thanks,' he replied, walking into the hallway and putting his bag down.

'I . . . er . . . need a favour, bro,' he said, looking down at his feet.

'You need that homework you missed last week?' I asked but he shook his head.

'Nah – it's kinda something else.'

'What?' I asked.

'Er . . . I was hoping . . . I need a place to stay, bro.'

I looked at him and I swear I saw tears in his eyes,

so I told him to come through to the living room. My head was going in all sorts of directions, trying to work out what was up. Jit sat down, looking even more embarrassed than before.

'Evenin',' said my gramps.

'Yeah . . . evenin',' replied Jit, quietly.

'You wanna tell me what's going on?' I asked.

Jit tried to smile at me but he couldn't. I heard my mum come through the door as I looked at my best mate.

'You best come upstairs,' I said, realizing that he wouldn't talk in front of my family.

My mum walked in and smiled at everyone. She saw Jit and grinned. 'Hi, Jit, how are you? I haven't seen you in ages.'

'Hi, Mrs Chambers,' he replied.

'Mum – me and Jit are gonna go upstairs for a chat. Is it OK if he stays for dinner?'

My mum smiled warmly. 'Of course it is, sweetheart.'

Normally I would have been embarrassed at her calling me sweetheart but I was too worried about Jit to care. Once we were in my room, I asked him what was up.

'My mum's been seein' this bloke and he don't like me so I don't want to go home,' he told me.

'What – has he been hitting you?' I asked, getting angry.

'Nah – nothing like that. He just gets drunk all the time and swears at me. Mum don't say nothing either.'

'That's messed up, bro,' I told him.

'Last night I didn't even go home,' Jit said, playing with his hands and not looking at me.

'You what? So where did you sleep?'

'In the park . . .'

I sat back in shock and more anger.

'Nah, nah, nah – that ain't happenin',' I said, shaking my head.

'I forgot my keys and Mum was at work. When I knocked on the door he told me to get lost. I walked around for ages and tried again about eleven but they didn't answer the door.'

'Didn't your mum notice you weren't there in the morning?' I asked.

'I never see her in the morning. She's always asleep because she works late and goes out and that.'

He saw the look in my eyes and shook his head.

'It ain't her fault, Dean. It's him . . . Micky. I just

don't wanna go home. I mean he let me in today but he threatened me, too. Told me he'd do me if I told Mum what happened . . .'

'Have you told your mum?' I asked.

Jit shook his head.

'I just grabbed some stuff and walked out. Mum's working till two in the morning anyway.'

'That's a nasty shift!'

'It's only 'cos the store opens twenty-four hours now . . . she used to finish at ten before and it ain't her fault,' he repeated.

I didn't know what else to say. I knew that things were hard for Jit but I didn't realize how bad. It kind of made me understand why he went nuts sometimes – I know I would have. I was so lucky to be close to my family. Sometimes it's easy to forget how lucky you really are. In the end I told him that we'd eat some food and that afterwards he should tell my mum.

'I don't wanna lie to her, bro – that ain't right,' I told him.

'OK,' he said, without complaining.

We *could* have lied and said that he was staying over because we had arranged it, but my mum can spot a lie from ten miles away. She's got this radar thing going on with her senses. And she would be hurt too. We went downstairs and sat in front of the telly as Gussie helped Ruby sort out the dinner. It was supposed to have been my turn but he didn't complain. Not in front of Mum, anyway.

We ate with my entire family, like we always did on Friday nights. My dad turned up around seven o'clock and by the time we sat down at the table, I was starving. Jit sat next to me and after a while he cheered up a bit, especially when my gramps started going on about his medical problems, like he always did.

'Yuh 'ave pepper sauce, Pearl?' he asked my mum.

She passed it across and Gramps opened it and poured it over his rice and chicken like he was pouring ketchup. My dad had bought the pepper sauce from the West Indies and it was extra hot, like a grenade going off in your mouth. But Gramps didn't even feel it. At one point he even put *more* on his food. I asked Jit if the food was nice, which was a stupid question because he was eating it so quickly that he must have liked it. He swallowed a mouthful and nodded.

''S'great,' he said. 'I like hot food.'

My dad laughed.

'You wanna try the pepper sauce, Jit – it's seriously hot.'

'Why's it called *Ooh Mi Raas!*,' I asked my dad, even though I knew what it meant.

'Not at the table, Clem,' said my mum.

'Why not?' asked Gussie. 'Gramps talks like that all the time and, anyway, it ain't rude.'

Gramps smiled at Jit.

'Mi used to 'ave one Indian fren a school, y'know.'

Jit looked at me and grinned.

'Really?' he said.

'Yeah, man – 'im name Guptal Patel – one wicked fas' bowler . . . im' coulda lick dung dem wicket.'

This time Jit looked confused.

'He's talking about cricket,' said my dad, as Gramps carried on eating, like he hadn't actually started a conversation.

'So . . . why *is* it called *Ooh Mi Raas!*,' asked Ruby. 'It's a stupid name for pepper sauce.'

'OK – seeing as Gramps hasn't brought up toilet humour at the table, I'll have to,' relented my mum, grinning like a kid.

'Yuh waan get a extra hot sauce, nex' time. Dis one

is a'right but it nuh keep yuh reg'lar like dem one in Jamaica.'

'It's from Antigua, Dad,' said my dad, winking at me and Jit.

'*Antigua?* Is dat why it 'ave such a stupid name?'

My dad started laughing.

'The name, if you translate it, means "Oh my arse!" because of the laxative effect that the peppers have,' he explained to Jit.

'It makes you crap yourself if you—' began my brother.

'*GUSSIE!*' shouted my mum, though she immediately cracked up along with everyone else, apart from Gramps.

'Is no wonder mi bone dem ache and mi 'ave piles,' said Gramps.

'*Ehhh, Gramps!*' said Ruby. 'That's nasty.'

Gramps smiled and winked at me and Jit.

'Jus' like yuh hairdo,' he whispered with a grin.

'*MUM!*' protested Ruby but my mum was laughing along too.

My dad watched Jit clear his plate and then asked him if he wanted some more.

'Yes please, Mr Chambers,' replied Jit, looking more than happy.

My dad took his plate and gave him a load more food, before filling up my plate and his own too. He picked up the bottle of sauce.

'You want some?' asked my dad.

'Er . . . nah – it's spicy enough for me,' said Jit.

'He don't wanna spend the rest of the evening in our shi—'

'Gussie, I told you – *shut it!*' said my mum.

'Course, back in my day a bwoi woulda get lick dung if 'im cheek 'im muddah so,' said Gramps.

'Don't worry about it, Gramps,' replied my mum, glaring at Gussie. 'It would still 'appen here too.'

'I was only jokin', Mum!' said Gussie.

'We neveh tell joke at de table,' started Gramps. 'Cah we would a get . . .'

'*Lick dung!*' said my dad, acting like a kid.

Gramps pulled out his lower set of false teeth and cleaned them with his forefinger before putting them back into his mouth. He shook his head, muttered to himself and carried on with his dinner.

Afterwards we told Mum about what was up with Jit

and she took him into the kitchen and spoke to him for ages as I watched telly with my sister. Dad and Gussie went off to work and Gramps was sitting in the front room listening to the BBC World Service on his old radio. When my mum and Jit returned, he was smiling and my mum told me that he was going to stay the night and that she'd phoned his mum at work to talk to her.

'Everything's going to be fine,' she told me, sitting down on the sofa.

'You OK, bro?' I asked Jit.

'Yeah – I spoke to Mum,' he said, smiling at me.

'So it's sorted?'

'Yeah – she's coming round tomorrow afternoon.'

'I've got some of that toffee ice cream,' said my mum. 'You want to get it out of the freezer, Dean?'

I smiled and went into the kitchen, relieved that my best mate was OK.

NINE

Jit was waiting for me outside his house the following Monday, looking happier than I'd seen him in ages. His mum had picked him up on the Saturday and spent half an hour chatting with my mum. She'd given her boyfriend the push, she said.

We walked down to Grace's as usual and caught the bus to school, all of us in a good mood, even though I hadn't done the poem for the school paper. It turned out that I didn't need to either because when I saw Hannah at registration she told me that the last article was going to be written by Mr Black.

'He's writing something about the football thing last week,' she told me. 'About racism and how to react to it properly.'

'Saved *my* skin,' I pointed out, but Hannah shook her head.

'Not exactly – he said that he still wants you to write it for the next one.'

'Yeah,' I replied, 'but that's not for a few weeks is it?'

'Gives you time to get on with it then,' said Hannah.

'No problem, Sister Aitch.'

I heard Grace yelp behind me and turned to find her bent over Jit's knee with her bag round her neck and her hair all over the shop.

'Yo, Jit – not in the classroom, bro,' I laughed.

'Ehh! What you two doin?' asked Suky.

'I was trying to get her bag,' said Jit, going all red, as Grace straightened herself up and stood there, looking like someone had painted her face with raspberry juice too.

'Er . . .' she began but Hannah just held up her hand.

'Don't even try to explain,' she said. 'I don't know what you were doing but there's laws, *y'know*?'

'OK – quiet everyone,' said Mrs Dooher.

'Miss! Grace and Jit are trying to make babies!' shouted a lad called Marco.

Mrs Dooher tried to look all serious but she couldn't manage it and she broke out into a grin.

'I'm sure they're not,' she told Marco.

'But I seen them – Grace was all over him,' added Marco's twin brother, Milorad.

'You saw them, Milorad. Not seen,' corrected Mrs Dooher.

'But I did seen, miss,' said Milorad.

'Oh – never mind – just keep quiet and pay attention. And, Grace, can you keep your hands to yourself until you're in your next lesson? I'd much rather Mr Herbert had to deal with this kind of thing.'

'I wasn't doing anything, miss,' Grace protested.

'Yeah – we were just messing about,' said Jit, before turning to Marco. 'I'm gonna batter you,' he said.

'*JIT!*' shouted Mrs Dooher.

'Oh I'm sorry, miss,' replied Jit, turning back to Marco. 'I shall jolly well bash you on the nose, my good fellow,' he told him, in a stupid voice.

'OK – enough. I'm too old for this rubbish.'

'Just think, miss,' said Hannah. 'If he'd have only asked you out, that Paul McFartney or whatever, when you were a young woman – you'd be rich and famous now.'

'Yes, yes, Hannah. Thank you for reminding me,' said Mrs Dooher, smiling warmly.

'Tropical islands, yachts. Your own chef ... just think,' continued Hannah.

'A *gun*,' added Mrs Dooher, jokingly.

Hannah said 'oops' and shut up.

I spent most of the morning thinking about who I was going to try and sell the mobile phones to. I'd decided to ask for seventy pounds for each of them, which I thought was the deal of the year considering that they were more than that in the shops. I'd brought one with me to school, and every few minutes I kept opening my bag and having a secret look at it. I didn't even tell Jit but I was going to eventually. I wanted to test the water. Do a bit of market research and that. My first option was trying a lad called Dilip who was in my class. His old man was loaded and they owned a load of fried chicken shops all over the city. He had a wicked phone already but I knew that I could tempt him with another one. Especially at the price I was giving him. I thought that I might even be able to sell him a couple of them – one for him and one for his brother, Nital, who was in the year above us. I finally got hold of Dilip at lunch, when he was standing in line for food. I went over as he was piling his plate high with chips. There was a slice of pizza underneath but it had been covered.

'Yes, Dilip – what a gwaan, blood?' I asked him, a big smile on my face.

Dilip looked around, like he didn't think that I was talking to him, even though I had used his name.

'You talkin' to *me,* guy?' he asked, in his whiny voice.

'Yeah, bro. How's it hangin', homeboy?'

'Safe, innit,' he told me, grabbing about ten sachets of ketchup.

I took a plate and put some chips on it, along with a piece of dry-looking chicken that was supposed to be tandoori. It was bright red, like that Ferrari colour, and as soon as it hit my plate, it left stains on the white surface. Nice. I was going to complain but I didn't. School dinners had got me into enough trouble already.

'Anyway, bro, I was *thinking,*' I said.

'Yeah?' replied Dilip.

'That *mobile* you got – it's kinda rude, man.'

For a moment Dilip looked worried, like I was about to tax his raas or something. I grinned at him, so that he'd calm down, and in my head I cussed him for thinking I was a thief. Talk about stereotype city, you get me?

'I ain't gonna *rob* you,' I told him. 'I just wondered if you was in the market for a new one, is all.'

Dilip shrugged.

'Happy with the one I got, Dean,' he told me.

'I'm happy with mine too but why settle for the *Ford Fiesta* when you can have the *Mercedes*?'

'You what?' he asked, looking puzzled.

'I got these killer things, man. BlackBerry with *everything* and open to every network. Dem tings open to some networks ain't even exist yet, you get me?'

'But I don't *want* a new phone,' he repeated.

'Listen – right *now* you don't want one but when one of the other kids gets one, then you'll feel bad. You gotta ask yerself what you is goin' to *be*, Dilip, my brother. A *leader* or a *follower*, you get me?'

Dilip walked off with his tray of food and I followed, sitting down next to him.

'I'm offering you the best on the market at a discount. At least have a look at it, nuh man.'

Dilip looked at one or two of the other lads at the table, all his friends, and then looked at me.

'Open to anything?' he asked.

I smiled. Just fling out the line and reel dem fishes in, I thought to myself.

'Every single one. I got them off a mate who owns a shop, man. Pure *legit*.'

'Lemme see then, bro,' he replied. I unzipped my bag and pulled out the phone, and straight away I could tell he wanted one. His eyes widened and lit up like there were floodlights behind them.

'*See?* Nice, innit?'

'Yeah, man . . . I seen one of these in the shop. Over a hundred.'

'Well then it's your lucky day, Dilip. I'm *only* asking *seventy*.'

'What's wrong with it?' asked Dilip, warily.

'Nuttin', man. I got another *five* waiting at home.'

'So why are they so *cheap*?' he said.

'End of line – stock clearance. My guy, Raj at Raj Electronics gave them to me.'

'That the shop on East Park Road?' asked Dilip.

'Yeah – that's the one – up the road from your dad's place.'

'I know him, so if they're dodgy, I'll find out,' he warned.

'Then what you got to *lose*? I'm kinda acting as his agent anyways,' I lied. 'He needs to shift some stock – *off the books*, you get me?'

I winked at him, like it was our big secret. The last bit made Dilip change his mind, I reckon. He smiled and told me about how his dad had to do things off the books sometimes.

'Get tax too much otherwise, innit,' he told me.

'So what you *saying* – we's looking out for the small *biznizz*, innit?' I replied, turning on the charm.

'OK, Dean – I'll get the money tomorrow but they better be all right.'

'Come, Dilip, man. Would I have your legs up?'

He thought about it for a minute and then told me he'd see me tomorrow.

'Ask around too, bro. Anyone else you know wants one – just send 'em my way. But keep it under wraps, man.'

He nodded.

'I'm serious, bro. Pure MI5 business a gwaan.'

I stood up and walked over to where Jit and Imtiaz were sitting, a big smile playing on my face. Damn, I was good, I told myself.

'What you smiling at?' asked Jit as I took my usual seat.

'Just thinking 'bout how I might have to go into stock-brokering or summat when I'm older . . .'

'Eh? You don't even like maths,' said Imi. 'How are you gonna sell stocks and shares?'

'Ain't about maths, is it?' I said, even though I didn't have a clue what I was on about.

'So what's it all about then?' asked Imi, getting on his high horse.

'You can either sell or you can't,' I told him. 'And I'm the daddy of salesmen, Imi. The bona fide, *numero uno*, you get me?'

'You eat summat funny?' asked Jit, giving me a strange look. 'Other than a dictionary, I mean.'

'I'll tell you later,' I said, as I saw Mr Herbert walk into the dining hall.

'YOW! HERBERT BWOI!!!' I shouted, leaning down under the table, so that he wouldn't see me.

Everyone in the hall stopped for a moment, waiting to see if someone would get into trouble. When nothing happened, they started talking again. I went further under the table, my knee slipping on a soggy chip that was on the floor.

'DUTTY HERBERT, BWOI! Is where you get that tie?' I shouted.

This time there was total silence. I thought about

not carrying on but the stupid part of my head beat up the sensible bit.

'The thing so nasty, it even make yuh mother cry!' I said, finishing my little rhyme.

'*WHO SAID THAT!*' bellowed Herbert, as the other kids started laughing.

I heard Jit snigger and stayed under the table, getting ready for the big finale. I put on a really deep voice.

'*FEE FI FO FUM . . . I smell a dutty Herbert man. Man so nasty he never cleans . . . Only polishes his head with Mr Sheen.*'

My voice had been amplified by being under the table and the whole hall went up in laughter, as I scrambled out from my hiding place and took my seat. As I did that Jit and Imi stood up so that I wouldn't get seen. Mr Herbert was so red in the face that he looked like a giant strawberry. He was looking in my direction too but in the end he stomped out of the hall because he couldn't prove that it had been me who'd dissed him.

'You're nuts, Dean,' laughed Imi.

'Least I got 'em,' I replied, grinning.

TEN

Dilip bought one of the phones the next day. I tried to sell him one for his brother but he told me that he was going to wait and see if his was OK first.

'Your loss,' I told him. 'Once in a lifetime bargain.'

Jit came up as he was walking away and asked me what I was up to.

'Sellin' phones, bro,' I told him.

I opened my bag and got out another one, handing it to him. He looked at it and whistled.

'Nice.'

'I got five left – you can have one if you like.'

'*Serious?*'

I grinned.

'Not to keep for yourself, you fool. I'm selling 'em for seventy notes. You sell that one, give me a tenner and you're laughing,' I said.

Jit looked over it a few more times.

'It's worth more than a tenner, bro,' he said.

'You're looking it in the mouth,' I replied.

'You *what*?'

'The Gift Horse.'

I don't know whether he got the joke but he smiled and said thank you.

'There's gotta be summat up with them, though.'

I shook my head.

'Nuttin'. Gussie got 'em from Raj – *you know*, the one that owns the phone shop?'

'Yeah – I know him – drives that big Audi.'

'Well he had to get rid of a few, off the books,' I said, before winking at him.

'*Cool.* Dunno who I'm gonna sell it to though. How many of the kids at school got seventy quid to play with?'

I smiled at him.

'*Plenty.* You's forgettin' all the posh kids that live round Grace's way.'

'Oh yeah,' he said, like he'd only just heard about them.

'That's where your skill as a salesman comes in,' I told him.

'Oh, that's what you was on about yesterday. I thought you'd been licking rock.'

'Never . . . and walk around like I'm from outer space? *Leave dat!*'

We chatted for a bit longer and then walked slowly towards our next lesson. Robert and Wesley were waiting outside the classroom when we got there, still talking about that lame book.

'So what's new with the Flute of Kings then?' I asked.

Robert shut up quickly and looked down at his feet but Wesley didn't realize that I was having a laugh.

'Tar, the talking rat, has turned to the Dark Way,' he said.

'Nah!' I said, pretending to be really shocked.

'I'm afraid so. He's taken the flute from the princess. She was sleeping and he stole in and spirited it away and now it's with the Dark Lord and—'

'What about Ganglefart the Goblin?' I asked.

Wesley looked at me strangely.

'I don't think that there is a Ganglefart, unless of course you've read more of it than me?'

'He's having a joke at our expense,' said Robert.

'*Oh dearie me,*' said Jit, sarcastically.

'I ain't,' I told them. 'I'm just exercising my

imagination – you know, making up my own characters and that.'

'Oh right,' said Wesley, looking at Robert.

'I suppose that's really rather clever,' admitted Robert. 'I never thought of that.'

'You should write your own,' I said.

I wasn't joking either. Not *completely*. Robert and Wesley had read every fantasy book going. They were like experts on good and evil, witches and sorcerers and that.

'I am,' said Robert, going red.

'What's it called?' I asked, as Jit pretended to yawn.

'It's a bit of a steal actually. I'm writing a further adventure of Princess Wondlebarn.'

'You mean Catwoman.'

'Well yes, I suppose. Only recently my visual image of the princess has changed somewhat.'

'Who to?' I asked, trying not to crack up.

'I'd rather not say,' he told me, going even redder than he already had and looking over my shoulder.

I turned to see Hannah and Grace walking towards us.

'*Hiya, boys*,' they said together, in American accents.

'Yo, sistas,' I replied. 'Roberto's writing a *book*.'

'*Are you?*' asked Grace in a silly, girlie voice. '*Really?*'

'Erm . . . well . . .' began Robert.

'He is,' Wesley replied for him. 'It's a fantasy and it's about—'

'Goblins and dwarves?' asked Grace.

'*Yes!*' said Robert, a bit too loudly.

'Excellent,' replied Grace. She held out her hand and touched Robert's sleeve, leaning towards his face. 'You will remember *liddle old moi* when you're rich, won't you?' she asked.

Robert pulled his arm away and I swear his legs were shaking. He looked at his friend before replying.

'Of . . . of . . . c-c-course,' he stuttered.

'Awfully *nice* of you,' said Grace, looking at Hannah, who seemed bored.

'Better go,' she said. 'Lovely to talk to you again, Roberto.'

Robert mumbled something back and walked off into class, with Wesley behind him. I looked at my friends and shook my head.

'You lot are so mean,' I told them.

'What? You started it,' said Jit. 'Talkin' nonsense and that.'

'I was being *nice*,' said Grace.

272

'Yeah, right. Like I believe you,' said Hannah.

'I *was*,' she protested. 'Those poor boys are always getting grief – I was just being friendly.'

'Bein' a div more like,' said Jit.

'Smelly, poo pants,' replied Grace, walking into the classroom.

Jit's face fell.

'She's only playing with you, Jit,' said Hannah, looking bemused. 'God, sometimes I wonder whether boys have got any brains at all.'

Jit sold the second phone as we were walking back to my house, later on. We were walking past a Caribbean takeaway that my aunt ran and as we turned the corner into a side street I heard someone say my name.

'Dean!' came the whisper.

'Easy, Dilip – what a gwaan?' I asked him, wondering why he was speaking so softly. Jit didn't bother to hold his thoughts in though.

'What you whisperin' for, you freak?' he asked loudly.

'I got someone else, innit. Wants a ting,' replied Dilip, looking embarrassed.

'What ting?' said Jit.

'A phone, bro . . .' Dilip told us.

I smiled and shook my head.

'See? Me done tell you you'd want another one . . .' I told him.

'Still can't see why you're whisperin' like a girl,' said Jit.

'But Dean said to keep it hush-hush, innit,' replied Dilip. 'I'm just bein' careful.'

'You sound like you're asking us for *drugs* or summat,' I said.

'Sorry, man,' replied Dilip, looking worried.

'Ain't no one around to hear us,' I said. 'We ain't in school, bro.'

Dilip looked sheepish and shrugged.

'Safe,' he said, once he was sure that no one was listening.

'We ain't sellin' crack, you tool,' said Jit, breaking all the rules of selling. You didn't call your potential customer names. I realized that I was going to have to step in to save the sale.

'Jit's got one,' I told Dilip. 'Same price as the other one.'

'Yeah . . . I got the notes on me,' said Dilip, still trying to keep his voice down.

I looked at Jit.

'*What?*' he said.

'The *phone*, Jit. Get the phone out, man.'

'Oh yeah,' replied Jit, catching on with the speed of a tortoise.

He pulled the phone and charger out of his bag and handed them to Dilip. Dilip waited for a moment and then held out his hand like he was going to shake Jit's.

'What you doin', you fool?' asked Jit.

'Givin' you the money, innit,' said Dilip.

Jit took what Dilip had in his hands. He had folded the notes into a tight little square and Jit had to straighten them out. I watched him do it and then decided to play a little joke.

'POLICE!' I shouted.

Dilip's face dropped and he looked like he had just pooped his pants, whilst Jit panicked and tried to shove the money down his trousers. Both of them were looking around for the police. When they realized that they were safe, they turned their attention to me. I just shrugged and grinned at them.

'Teach you not to be paranoid,' I said, shaking my head. 'Fools.'

Dilip put the phone in his bag and told us he was going.

'Later,' I said, just as my auntie came out of her shop.

'*DEAN!*' she shouted at the top of her voice. 'Is what you doin' messin' 'bout outside my business?'

'Hi, Auntie Sandra,' I said.

'Better not be doin' nuttin' wrong,' she told me, before eyeing up Jit. 'Who ah dis?' she asked.

'This is my best mate, Jit,' I told her.

'You wan' come in an' nyam some food?' she asked, smiling now.

'An' get beat up by me mum for not eatin' at home? *Nah* – I'll check you another time, Auntie,' I told her.

'Anytime,' she said, looking round and then cussing a wino who was sitting on the pavement, across the street. '*Eeedjat!*' she called to him, before going back into her shop.

ELEVEN

Things started to go wrong the next day. I was walking from History to English when I felt a hand grab my jumper from behind. My legs started buckling as I got dragged backwards into the toilets. When the hands let go of me, I straightened myself out and turned to see Jason Patel grinning at me. He's a weird looking geezer, Jason, with red hair and red freckles on light, almost yellow skin. His nose is too long for his face and his eyes are like little piggy things and when he smiles, he's seriously ugly. I'm talking scare-the-living-poo-out-of-a-serial-killer butt ugly. I looked at him for a moment and then glanced away, my eyes hitting the floor.

'What did I tell you?' he asked, poking me in the chest with his finger.

Now there's some things I can handle, like being punched or kicked. You know that's going to hurt and you get it over with. But when Jason poked me in the chest I started to get really angry. It didn't hurt, it just stung a little bit, but it was so irritating. And then he did it over and over again. I was dying to hit him but I knew that if I did he would batter me, good and proper. In the end, I played the tough nut and just shrugged at him.

'Dunno,' I said.

'WHAT DID I TELL YOU?' he shouted, making me flinch.

'Summat 'bout not sellin' nuttin' or summat?' I replied.

'Exactly,' he said, calming down a bit. 'And what do I hear you been doing?'

'Sellin' stuff . . .' I admitted.

'Yep – so either you don't care 'cos you is so hard or you is trying to diss me, bro!' he said.

'Nah . . . I just forgot,' I said, trying to style it out. Yeah, right.

Jason grabbed my jumper and head-butted the side of my face. He would have butted my nose but I turned my head. My ear was stinging and I felt light-headed but I didn't fall over or cry. I just stood my ground.

'You won't forget that,' he told me, grabbing my bag from my shoulder and opening it. I didn't try to stop him – I'm not that stupid.

He rummaged around before pulling out one of the phones. Luckily I had only brought one with me. He would have taken the lot otherwise.

'That'll do,' he said.

'It's seventy notes,' I told him.

'Yeah,' he grinned. 'I'll write you a cheque.'

'But they don't belong to me,' I said quickly, without thinking. 'They belong to this man up East Park Road.'

'*And?*' he asked, grinning again, his face creasing like someone had squashed his head.

'Well, he's gonna want his money.'

'You threatening me?' he asked, his grin disappearing.

'Nah . . . I'm just sayin' that the bwoi is gonna want his dough.'

Jason looked at the phone and then back at me.

'Tell him that he can ask me himself,' he said, acting all brave.

'OK, then,' I said.

He turned to go, throwing my bag to the floor, but

then he stopped, walked back to me and slapped me on the same ear that he'd butted.

'Next time you'd better listen to me,' he said, before walking out.

I grabbed my bag and walked into one of the cubicles, locked the door and tried to calm down. What was I going to do about Jason?

In the end, I didn't tell anyone about what Jason had done. I decided that it would be easier to leave it and get my own back some other way. It was the right decision too, only I didn't know it at the time. I sold the last three phones over the next few days, and when I counted up the money, along with the tenner that Jit gave me for his phone, I'd made two hundred and ninety quid. It would have been more but for Jason Patel. Still, it was a lot of money and I decided that I was going to buy an Xbox with it. I'd always wanted one and I told Gussie that he was going to have to cover for me when it arrived, so that my mum wouldn't get funny about where the money had come from. Gussie agreed. I rang Jit on the Friday night and told him to come round for dinner. He turned up about two minutes after I'd put the phone down, with an overnight bag.

'Mind if I stay over?' he asked, putting his bag down on my bed.

'Looks like you've already decided for me,' I said, smiling. 'It's cool.'

'What's for food?' he asked, looking excited.

'Same as last time, I think.'

'Wicked!' replied Jit.

'Come – let's eat and then we got some *research* to do on the internet, bro.'

Jit gave me a strange look.

'What for?'

'I'm buying an Xbox,' I told him.

'Xbox?'

'Yeah. We can share it though!'

Jit thought about it for a moment and then smiled at me.

'Gets better and better,' he said.

Gramps spent the entire meal telling us about the time that he saw a bloke called Prince Buster, whilst he was making some old Ska tunes or something. Ska's like the first version of reggae music, I think, but I didn't ask. I just nodded along, as Gramps told us about this girl they used to call *Mash-Mout Lorna* because she had no teeth. My sister, whose middle name is Lorna, was going mental because me and Gussie were ripping her about it. In the end, my dad told us to stop because she was about to run out of the room. Gramps didn't even notice. Instead he told us about meeting Bob Marley instead. I reckon he makes up half of his stories about Jamaica but I don't care because they're normally *well* funny.

After dinner, me and Jit had to load up the dishwasher and then we grabbed a drink each and headed up to my room. I sat at my PC and hit Google. Then I typed 'Cheap Xbox' into the search panel. The page came up in about half a second and I started to read down the list of online shops, reading out the little promotional lines to Jit. After a few minutes, I clicked one of the links and the page for the shop appeared. As soon as it was done, I realized that I had a problem. You can't buy online with cash. I told Jit, who just shrugged and took the mouse from me, clicking on a picture of some really expensive special edition Xbox.

'We can't get that,' I told him. 'It costs too much – I've got two twenty max.'

'I thought you had more dough than that?' asked Jit.

'Yeah, I have,' I told him, 'but I don't wanna spend

it all, bro. There's other things I need to keep it for.'

'Cool,' said Jit. 'You can put a maximum spend amount in this box here.' He pointed it out with the mouse.

'I've gotta go talk to Gussie first,' I said, getting out of my seat. Jit jumped straight in.

'Cool – I'll just check out a few options,' he said, like he was some kind of shopping expert.

I went downstairs to find Gussie, who had the night off from my dad's bar. He was in the lounge, lying on the sofa watching rubbish on the telly.

'I need a favour, bro,' I told him.

He looked at me for a bit and then turned his attention back to the TV.

'Gussie?'

'What?'

'I need to borrow your debit card ting . . .'

'You what?' he said, sitting up. 'Is what kind of nonsense yuh chat 'bout?'

I pulled the wad of notes out and showed them to him.

'Not for nuttin',' I told him. 'I've got the money.'

'*Raas*,' said Gussie, in surprise. 'That all from them phones?'

'Yeah,' I said, suspiciously. 'You said I could do what I wanted with them.'

Gussie grinned.

'Relax, man. I don't want a bigger cut, baby bro. What do you need my card for?'

I told him and he nodded, telling me that he would lend me his card. I gave him the cash which he put in his back pocket.

'Is there enough money in your account?' I asked.

'*Yeah, bro* – me have money, y'know. Besides it's the least I can do considering.'

Only, I didn't think about the last thing he said because I was already turning to run back upstairs, excited about getting the Xbox. Bad move.

Jit was still looking at the PC when I got back. I took my seat from him and went into another online shop and then another, trying to find the best deal. In the end we settled on an Xbox plus four game deal. I entered Gussie's card details as quickly as I could. It was quick delivery too, which meant that it'd probably arrive by Monday. I was well excited, so much that I forgot all about Jason Patel. Instead we played on my other console until about two in the morning.

TWELVE

The next day me and Jit went round to Grace's in the afternoon. Hannah was already there and we chilled out for a couple of hours, playing pool and talking rubbish. Hannah was trying to get us to think about ideas for the next school paper but we ignored her. Grace was in her usual weirdo mood, talking about rabbits and their poo.

'They eat their own poo,' she said, just as I was about to sink the black ball and beat Jit's sad ass for the fifth time. It put me right off my shot and the ball cannoned off three cushions.

'Eurgh!' I said.

'That's nasty!' added Jit, screwing up his face.

'They do, though,' said Grace, grinning.

'No they don't,' replied Hannah. 'I used to have one – I know.'

'You obviously don't,' said Grace. 'Rabbits have

something like seventeen thousand taste glands or something and humans only have ten thousand.'

'Easy, Sister Gee,' I said. 'You sound like you're doin' a documentary.'

'It's true. When they poo, some of the nutrients and stuff are still in it and they eat it to get the rest out.'

'That's why I ain't never havin' no pets,' said Jit.

'Duttyness,' I said.

'I used to kiss my bunny,' said Hannah.

'*NAH! You dutty raas!*' I shouted.

'Not *really*,' said Hannah, getting embarrassed.

'You're *gonna* say that now,' Jit told her.

'I was *joking*,' she replied.

'Hannah kiss the bunny with botty breath . . . *nah*!' I continued, until Hannah picked up a spare cue and came towards me.

'Easy, Sister Aitch, I was only playing,' I said, pretending to be scared.

'I'm gonna shove this up your ar—'

'Well, this is becoming rather familiar,' said Mr Parkhurst from the foot of the stairs.

Hannah looked at him and said, 'Oh my God.'

'You seem to have a thing about Dean and that cue,' said Mr Parkhurst.

The rest of us cracked up while Hannah went red. Again.

'Anyone fancy a coffee?' asked Grace's dad.

'*Yeah!*' said Jit, like a little kid. 'Can I help you make it?'

'Of course you can, Jit,' replied Mr Parkhurst.

Jit followed him upstairs as Grace turned to me and Hannah and mimicked her dad.

'*Of course you can, Jit – why not be a bumlick while you're at it?*' she whispered in a childish voice.

'Like Hannah and the bunny?' I said.

'*DEAN!*' shouted Hannah, grabbing the cue again.

We went out about an hour later, after Grace's dad made us promise to stay for tea. We walked down past a row of shops and then cut across to the main road that led into the city. From there we walked to Queens Road, where we stopped at a shop to buy chocolate because Grace said that she would die if she didn't have some. Jit waited outside for us and when we returned he looked amazed.

'What?' I asked him.

'You look like someone just shot you,' said Hannah.

'Look over the road,' said Jit, pointing to a news-agent's.

'*What?*' asked Grace. 'It's a shop.'

'They're *in* the shop,' said Jit.

'Who, gimpy boy?' asked Hannah.

'Imi and Suky,' replied Jit.

'Ooh, cool,' said Grace. 'I need to talk to Suky about some homework.'

'*Nah*,' said Jit. 'You don't get me. They're in there together.'

'So?' I asked, starting to get bored.

'*TOGETHER* . . . like, holding hands!' he replied.

'*NO!*' said Grace and Hannah together.

'Yep – seen them with my own eyes. They were holding hands.'

Hannah and Grace pulled us back into the shop we had just come out of.

'What you doin', you divs?' I shouted.

'*SSSH!*' said Grace. 'They'll hear you when they come out.'

'And?'

'We *don't* want them to *see* us,' said Hannah, like that was supposed to make sense.

'Let's follow them!' said Grace.

'No. Let's do something really interesting like watch our feet grow,' said Jit.

'Oh shut up, farty pants,' said Grace.

'*Oh my God there they are!*' said Hannah, as though she'd seen a movie star.

'*Hide!*' said Grace, pulling me and Jit further back into the shop, just as an old man was trying to get out. He tut-tutted at us and walked off mumbling.

'Silly old man,' said Grace.

Across the street, Imi and Suky walked up towards some traffic lights. They didn't have a clue that they were being watched and they didn't look like they cared, holding hands and stopping to kiss each other every few moments. It was like something out of a chick flick. Grace waited until they had turned a corner before walking out of the shop.

'Come on!' she said to the rest of us. 'Let's see where they go.'

We spent the next hour and a half following Imi and Suky, as they walked in some kind of strange zigzag pattern back towards the area they lived in, which was near Grace's house. They took the long way round to everywhere and a couple of times we had to duck and hide behind hedges and stuff so that they wouldn't spot us. At first it was OK, because it was like we were on a secret mission or something, but eventually it just got really boring and I was getting hungry too. So was Jit, who moaned like a five-year-old, which was also the way that Grace and Hannah were acting. They were giggling to each other and talking about how they were going to tease Suky on Monday.

'She told us that she thought he was *ugly*,' said Hannah.

'To put you off her trail, prob'ly,' I replied.

'Cheeky moo,' said Grace. 'And *he* said that he didn't fancy her at all – the little liar.'

'What did you expect them to say with you witches on their case? I don't get what the big deal is, myself,' I replied.

'Idiot,' said Hannah, matter-of-factly. 'It's all about group dynamics.'

'Is that food?' asked Jit. 'Only I'm gonna faint if I don't eat soon.'

'No one,' began Grace, ignoring Jit, 'in our little group has crossed the line between friendship and romance until now. It's bound to change the way things work.'

'How we all relate to each other,' added Hannah.

'You been reading too many of them stupid magazines,' I said. 'I'm not gonna start bein' different with you two just because them two can't stop licking each other's faces.'

'Yeah,' said Jit, before glancing at Grace and then looking away. I don't know why he was trying to take my side. It was obvious he was mad about her.

'See what we mean?' said Hannah.

'Nah . . .' I lied.

'It'll be you and Hannah, soon enough,' said Grace, winking at Jit.

'Leave it,' said Hannah.

'Get off that, man. You'd love to go out with me – I am the dan . . . how many times you gotta hear it, sista.'

As Suky and Imi got closer to their own houses they let go of each other's hands and started to act normally again. We followed them right up to Imi's road and then we turned and headed back for Grace's. Someone was going to get maximum grief on Monday, I thought to myself, before I let my mind fill with the images of food. Fat cheeseburgers with mustard and ketchup, greasy fried chicken and chips with hot pepper sauce, lamb kebabs like the ones from Picnic Kebab House on Evington Road, packed with salad and chillis and that fried haloumi cheese thing that my mum gets from the supermarket. Only when we got to Grace's, it was vegetable lasagne and home-made garlic bread. Not that I was complaining though. I was so hungry I would have eaten Jit if I could.

THIRTEEN

The following Monday, Grace wasn't at the bus stop when me and Jit got there and when we got to school she was already gossiping about Imi and Suky with everyone in our class. Suky and Imi weren't there when we arrived. They'd been sent to pick up some stuff for Mrs Dooher and when they returned everyone went quiet for a moment. Then Marco and Milorad whistled and the whole class went mad. Imi went red and sat down but Suky stood where she was, looking confused.

'You got seen!' shouted Puspha, talking to Suky.

'All kissy face and holding hands,' added Heather, as Dilip and Raj turned to face Imi.

'*Nah* . . . Imi's got a *girlfriend*!' they said, like little girls.

I didn't get what the big deal was. If they wanted to check each other that was cool with me – I mean we were getting old and that. The problem, as my sister once told me, was that some of us were more mature than the others, and Dilip and Raj were like, six, compared to me.

'Did you hold her hand?' asked Raj, grinning.

'Did she kiss you first or was it the other way round?' asked Heather.

'All right, all right . . . You sound like you're doing a rehearsal of *Grease*,' said Mrs Dooher. She had a little smile on her face when she said it.

'What's *Grease*?' asked Marco.

'You've got it all over your face, you dutty raas,' said Jit.

'*Miss!*' squealed Marco.

'*SHUT UP!*' shouted Mrs Dooher.

Everyone quietened down but they were still whispering to each other as Mrs Dooher took the register. I turned to Imi and smiled. 'Nice one, bro, although you could have let me know,' I told him.

'Shut up, Dean,' replied Imi, looking well vexed.

'Nah . . . I ain't joking. If you and Suky wanna bump uglies – that's none of my business, bro!'

'How did the *whole* class find out anyway?' he asked me.

'You'll have to ask the blabber mouths,' I told him, nodding towards Hannah and Grace who were talking to Suky and giggling again.

'I should have known,' he said, before smiling.

'So you two serious and that?' I asked.

'S'pose,' he replied.

'You kept that quiet,' added Jit, joining in.

'That's because I knew the whole school would find out about it,' he told us.

'So what? Ain't like you should care,' I said.

'I don't. Just didn't want the gossip,' said Imi, acting all mature. Like he'd never gossiped about anyone.

'Your parents mind that she's Sikh and you're Muslim?' asked Jit.

Imi shrugged.

'You ain't told 'em,' he said, 'I bet you let go of her hand when you reach the end of your road and that.'

Imi gave him a funny look. 'NO!' he said, defensively. 'What you know about it anyway?'

'I just do,' said Jit. 'There's that whole family honour thing, ain't there?'

'Not with my family,' said Imi.

'Least not until you tell 'em,' I said, grinning.

'Suky's family might not like it,' he said.

'Really?' I asked, but he turned away and shrugged.

'You'll have to ask her, bro,' he told me, like he'd said too much.

'I gettit – it's cool,' I told him.

'Can we talk about something else?' asked Imi, looking at Jit.

'Yep,' said Jit. 'How about rabbits?'

'You *what*?'

'*Rabbits*, bro. They eat their own poo,' replied Jit, smiling.

Imi looked at me and then back at Jit. 'You two need to get a life,' he said.

'Maybe a girlfriend too,' grinned Jit.

It went on like that all morning with Jit taking every opportunity to rip Imi. In the end, it got boring and I walked off to find Misha, who was in the year above us and fine. I wanted to get her phone number but didn't have the guts to ask for it. Not that I got the chance. I was walking down the main corridor, heading for the rear of the building, when Dilip caught up with me.

'Bro,' he called out.

I turned and saw him standing behind me, looking sheepish again.

'Easy, Dilip,' I said.

'Got a problem, innit?' he told me.

'Yeah?' I replied.

'Them tings gone funny,' he said.

'You what?'

'Them phones gone barred.'

For a minute I was about to smile, but then what he said sunk in and I felt my stomach knot. The phones were dodgy and I'd spent all the money on an Xbox.

I stood and thought quickly, before trying to talk my way out of it.

'Sold as seen,' I told him.

'Huh?' said Dilip, looking confused.

'Like when you buy stuff at a car boot sale, mate. No refunds, my brother.'

'But it don't work,' he said, his voice breaking a bit.

'Ain't my fault,' I said, trying to act brave.

Secretly though I was feeling bad. I mean I liked selling stuff and making money but I wasn't a con man or nothing. I wouldn't have sold the phones if I'd known that they didn't work. And that's when I remembered Gussie saying 'that's the least I can do . . .' after I'd asked to use his debit card.

'I w-want my money b-back,' stammered Dilip.

'No way, José,' I said. 'I ain't got it no more.'

'But—'

I had to think quickly so I said the first thing that came into my head.

'Tell you what – let me talk to my mate Raj tonight. I'll get him to sort them out – can't say fairer than that.'

Dilip looked at me and shrugged.

'OK,' he said.

'I didn't know they was dodgy,' I told him. 'Honestly, bro. I wouldn't do that.'

'You gonna speak to Raj then?' he asked.

'I just said so, didn't I? Check me tomorrow and I'll sort it,' I said, walking away in a real hurry.

I went over to one of the other buildings, ignoring Misha and her mates. I didn't have time for chatting up no sisters. I had to think quick. I headed for the toilets. Pushing open the door, I saw Paresh Solanki at the mirror, straightening his greasy hair.

'I wanna talk to you, Dean,' he said to me.

'Get lost, Paresh,' I said. 'I got things to do.'

He pulled out one of the phones.

'Yeah, you have. Like giving me back my money for this phone,' he said.

I looked at him like he was holding a stick of dynamite or something. I hadn't sold him a phone.

'Where'd you get that?' I asked.

'Dilip got it for me,' he said.

'I didn't know you and Dilip was mates,' I said.

'Cousins,' he told me.

'Well, like I just told him – I'm sorting it out later. Check me tomorrow and I'll get it unbarred.'

Paresh came closer to me.

'You better,' he said.

Even though he was older than me, I wasn't scared of him. It's not like he was Jason Patel. And then I remembered the phone that Jason took.

'You listening to me?' asked Paresh.

'Yeah, yeah,' I replied, trying not to let the fear show on my face. Jason was going to go mad – even though he'd never paid for the phone. I just knew what he was like.

'I'll find you tomorrow, then,' said Paresh, walking out into the corridor.

I sat in the cubicle after he'd gone and thought about how I was going to murder my brother. Then, as the bell went for the afternoon lessons, I sneaked my way through the school, praying that I didn't bump into Jason or anyone else that I'd sold a phone to. I made it to my next lesson in one piece and sat quietly at the back as Mrs Lee-Cross tried to explain something about fractions. The only fractions on my mind were the ones I'd be in when Jason got hold of me. I sneaked to my last lesson too, using Jit as cover, and I explained what was going on. Jit looked worried.

'But I ain't got the money no more,' he said.

'I know . . . but that ain't gonna help us.'

'Your brother should sort it out – it's his fault!' said Jit.

'Oh, believe it,' I said. 'When I get home, I'm gonna go mad!'

'He'll have to get Raj to sort 'em out,' said Jit.

'Yeah – only Raj is gonna charge.'

'Nah! I didn't think of that,' said Jit.

'And we ain't got the money . . . the Xbox, remember . . . ?'

'Can't we cancel the order?' asked Jit.

I shook my head.

'It's getting delivered today. Probably already at my house.'

'Raas . . .' replied Jit.

I didn't tell him about Jason though and I knew that Jason was going to be my biggest headache. After school I was standing with Imi and Jit, waiting for the bus when the inevitable happened.

'*OI! DEAN!*' came Jason's voice, just as the bus was pulling up and it started to rain. I was about to get on board, but realized that Jason would catch up. My only hope was to do a runner.

'*I'm gone!*' I told Jit and Imi, who had just bought their tickets.

I jumped through the open doors, passed the other kids and splashed through the rain, running as fast as I could. I could hear Jason shouting after me as I ran, my heart pounding . . .

FOURTEEN

'You look like a drowned rat,' said my brother, as I stood shivering in the doorway to our living room.

'There's only one rat round here, bro,' I replied, giving him the dirtiest look I could manage.

'What's up wit' you?' he asked.

I dumped my bag on the floor and rubbed my hand across my wet head.

'You ain't got *no* shame, have you?'

Gussie, who'd been lying on the sofa in front of the telly, sat up and scratched his head.

'The phones?' I said.

'Oh . . . yeah, I was gonna . . .' he began but I didn't give him the chance to finish what he was saying.

'You *knew* them phones was dodgy and you let me sell 'em. Now I've gotta get them all sorted and I've spent the dough on the Xbox and you knew all the time that they was—'

'It came,' said Gussie.

'*WHAT?*' I asked him, getting angrier.

'The Xbox, bro. Arrived this morning. I've even set it up for you and everything.'

'I don't give a toss 'bout the Xbox! You ripped me off. I'm your *brother*.'

Gussie shrugged then grinned at me.

'No worries, bro. I'll speak to Raj,' he said.

'I'm gonna get *murdered* when I get back to school and all you can do is smile at me, you t'ief.'

He gave me a funny look.

'Who's gonna murder you?' he said.

'This lad at school, Jason Patel, took one of the phones and I've just had to run all the way home 'cos he was after me and I'm gonna get battered and all you can do is . . .' I said, running out of breath before I could finish.

'Ease up, rude bwoi . . . ain't no one gonna batter you,' said my brother. 'Who's this Jason Patel anyway?'

'Just some lad from Year Ten.'

'Well forget about him – if he touches you I'll break his legs.'

'What about the rest of 'em? They all want their money back,' I said.

Gussie grinned again.

'I'll sort it,' he told me. 'I'm sorry, man. Raj told me they was OK.'

'That's why you let me have them for next to nothing, is it?' I was glaring at him.

'All right – so I knew that they might get barred but I didn't—'

'You're bang out of order,' I said.

'And you sound like your lines was written by someone on *EastEnders*,' he replied.

'Go stick your head up a cat's backside!'

'Leave it, bro. I said I'll sort it out. Let me give Raj a call.'

He pulled out his mobile and dialled a number, gesturing to a bag by his feet.

'More games – PlayStation and Xbox. I got 'em for you to sell,' he said, before talking to whoever answered the phone.

As he went through it all with Raj I looked at the games and then went to find a towel to dry off with. I was feeling a bit better, especially after Gussie had said that he'd take care of Jason. Only I was still recovering from being chased half the way home and I wasn't about to forget that my own brother had ripped me off. I walked back into the living room to find Gussie lying down again.

'*So?*' I asked.

'Sorted . . . he's gonna take the bar off 'em. Just tell whoever you sold them to that he'll do it for a tenner.'

'But they ain't gonna pay for that,' I said. 'They've already paid for them.'

'They's still getting a *bargain*, man. Them things are top dollar!'

'But I'm gonna get beat up,' I said.

'Tell them that it's better than a kick in the teeth, which is what they'll get if they touch you.'

'But . . .' I began.

Gussie shook his head at me. 'You tell them, man, that if they wanna get funny, they can come see me. Tell 'em that I've got their money.'

I thought about it for a moment and then nodded. 'OK,' I said.

'And meanwhile you can off-load them games in the bag . . . keep the money.'

'What's wrong with them?' I asked, learning my lesson fast.

'Nothing, man. It's just games, you get me?'

'But no one's gonna want them!'

'You ain't even tried yet,' said Gussie.

'But—'

'Bro, just get out of my face. I've sorted out the phones – what else do you want? Go play on your Xbox or summat.'

I mumbled a few swear words under my breath and went up to my room. When I saw the Xbox I cheered up a bit and thought about calling for Jit. He'd want to know why I had run off anyway and besides we had a new toy to play with. I even forgot about Jason as I put on my favourite game. I called for Jit about an hour after dinner and I told him all about why Jason had chased me. In the end I stopped worrying, remembering what Gussie had said about sorting him out. But if I thought that my troubles were over, I was wrong.

Next morning, Jit didn't turn up again. I made it to school without seeing anyone that I'd sold a phone to. Jason was still out to get me and Gussie couldn't help me in school, so I still had to be careful. I saw Dilip and told him all about the deal with Raj, and to begin with he wasn't having any of it.

'Nah, bro – I paid the money already,' he

whispered, as Mrs Dooher called the register.

I remembered what Gussie had said to me and repeated it. 'You're still getting the bargain of the century, man. It's only another tenner.'

'I dunno, bro.'

'Well, if you want your dough back you need to go see my brother,' I told him.

It did the trick. He mumbled something about never buying anything from me again and turned his back. But I prodded his shoulder so that he'd turn back around.

'And tell Paresh too. If he wants to get tough he can do it with my bro, you get me?'

Dilip went red and turned away again. I didn't feel pleased though. It wasn't my fault that the phones were dodgy and I didn't want to upset my school mates. I didn't want them going round telling everyone that I was shady and that. That was the kind of reputation I could do without.

'What you talkin' 'bout, sexy boy?' asked Grace.

'Nuttin',' I said, lying.

'I didn't realize that you and Dilip were such good friends,' she said.

'We're not.'

'Oh . . . must be my imagination,' said Grace, grinning.

The door slammed open and Jit hurried in, looking like he had been dragged through a hedge backwards.

'Yes, scarecrow!' said Imi, as Jit sat down.

'Jit . . . can I see you after registration,' said Mrs Dooher, not even looking up from what she was doing.

'Oops,' said Hannah.

'What's up wit' you?' I asked him.

'Jus' late,' he said.

One side of his face looked a bit swollen. Grace noticed, too.

'Someone hit you?' she asked, looking all concerned.

Jit looked at me and shrugged.

'Jason,' he said. 'He told me to give you a message.'

'Why would Jason hit—' began Hannah.

'Nuttin',' I said. 'We'll sort it out later.'

I gave Jit a look that said don't talk about it any more and he nodded at me.

'You boys are silly,' Grace told us. 'That's twice in

two weeks that Jason's beat up Jit. Just tell someone.'

'Don't worry,' I said, angrily. 'I'm going to – just as soon as I see that bwoi myself.'

'Ooh, hard man,' laughed Hannah.

'Just watch this space, Sister Aitch,' I replied.

FIFTEEN

I didn't see Jason for a couple of days. I did have to fend off the other people I'd sold phones to though. No one was happy about having to pay extra but I managed to get out of it pretty easily. The problem was that everyone found out about the dodgy phones which meant that I was having serious trouble selling anything else. All my usual customers were keeping well away. Every time I saw Dilip, he just ignored me and whispered stuff to his mates. I was like a leper. Kids were avoiding me in the corridor and pointing at me when I walked past but it wasn't all to do with the phones. Eventually Hannah told me that she'd overheard some of the lads in our class talking about me.

'They said that Jason is after your blood,' she said, looking worried.

I tried to shrug it off. 'He's always after me or Jit – nothing new there, sister.'

'This is serious, Dean. Those lads were laughing and talking about how Jason has been spreading it around that he's going to batter you.'

I still hadn't asked Gussie for help and I wondered whether I should. Only, I knew that I'd get called a grass if I did. People would think that I couldn't take care of myself and the other bullies in school would start to pick on me too. At least that's what I thought. I decided that it would all blow over anyway. I hadn't seen Jason so he couldn't have been that bothered, I said to myself. I was wrong about that too, though.

'You're nuts,' Hannah told me.

'Let him come,' I said, trying to act all hard. 'He don't bother me.'

She shook her head.

'One of these days,' she replied, 'you're going to get yourself into something that you can't talk your way out of.'

I grinned. 'Never. I could talk my way out of anything . . . Besides, them bullies want you to be scared of 'em. They don't like it when you aren't.'

'I still don't understand *why* he's after you though,' said Hannah, as Grace walked up.

'Who's after who?' she asked.

'Jason. He's telling people that he's going to beat Dean up.'

'Do you want me to knee him where it hurts?' asked Grace, jokingly.

'I wish that would help,' I admitted.

'So, why is he after you?' asked Hannah.

'Nuttin' really – just some stuff about a phone that don't work.'

I told them the whole story. After I'd finished, Grace shook her head at me.

'You aren't supposed to do that at school anyway,' she told me.

'Who cares?' I replied.

'Dean! Jason is a nasty piece of work,' she told me.

'Yeah,' added Hannah. 'I don't want my favourite boy getting beaten up over something so silly.'

'Easy,' I replied, grinning. 'So now I'm your favourite boy?'

'You know what I mean,' said Hannah. 'Stop being a fool.'

'But what about Jit?' I continued. 'He'll be jealous.'

'See what I mean?' said Hannah, looking angry. 'Stupid boy!'

'Silly, macho, too-much-testosterone-in-your-pants,

smelly, rabbit-poo-eating boy,' added Grace.

'Take a breath, Sister Gee,' I told her. 'You'll do yourself some damage.'

They told me to get lost and walked off. I just stood and shook my head. Girls are some funny things.

Jit wasn't around when I caught the bus home and I spent the journey wondering where he had got to. As the bus turned down Evington Road, I watched a group of kids make their way downstairs. My stop was further up the road, just before the bus headed into the city centre. I decided to go to the shops though. It was beginning to rain as I got off, jumping past Marco and Milorad.

'Watch it!' said Marco.

'Sorry, bro,' I replied, skidding on the wet pavement and colliding with Misha and one of her friends.

'Stupid knob!' shouted her mate, but Misha just stood and grinned at me.

'Hey, Misha – what you doin?' I asked, stupidly.

'Whaddya think I'm doin?' she replied, still smiling.

'Goin' home?'

'That's what I usually do after school.'

'Oh right. So, like, what are you . . .' I began again, not really knowing what I was going to say.

'This bwoi stupid, y'know,' said Misha's mate.

'No I ain't,' I said.

The girl held her hand in my face, just like my sister does, and turned her head away.

'Fool!' she said.

'Did you wanna ask me something, Dean?' said Misha.

I did. I wanted her phone number but my stomach knotted up and I couldn't think of anything to say. Nothing clever anyway.

'Er . . .'

'See?' said her friend. 'Stupid bwoi can't even talk properly.'

They walked off giggling and left me standing in the rain with my ego seriously bruised. I was the lyrics officer, and I couldn't even ask the girl for her digits. I needed to have a serious chat with myself.

I didn't feel bad for too long though. I crossed the road, running around the cars that were held up in a traffic jam and walked into an off-licence.

'Twenty B&H,' I said to the man behind the counter, as a joke.

'You know you ain't old enough,' said the bloke, whose name was Hardev.

'OK – you got me, bro. I'll just take a gallon of vodka and ten cigars.'

Hardev smiled and shook his head. 'You gonna buy anything, Dean?'

I nodded. 'Yeah, man. Just you looked kinda bored so I thought I'd come cheer you up,' I said.

'Buy the shop and let me go live on a beach somewhere,' replied Hardev, who had gone to school with my brother.

'How much you want? I got one pound and twenty-three old English pennies in me hand,' I told him.

He grinned again.

'Get out of it, you likkle raas!'

I picked up a bar of chocolate and gave him the right money.

'What kind of way is that to treat your best customer?' I said.

'I'll give you the back of my hand in a minute,' said Hardev, as I walked out the door.

The chocolate went down in two mouthfuls and as I crossed East Park Road, I decided that I wanted another one. There was a twenty-four hour shop further up the road and I walked in, past a couple of fit student girls, and headed for the sweet aisle. As I turned into it though I came face to face with the dog's backside that was Jason Patel's face.

'Who we got here then?' he said, smiling.

I didn't stop to think. I grabbed a handful of chocolates and shoved them in his face, pushing him into a display. He went flying and as I ran out, the guy behind the counter swore in an African language and went mad. I took a right down the side of the shop and sprinted away. Behind me, I heard Jason swearing and realized that he was on my tail. I ducked left into a second side street and raced to the end, where it joined St Stephen's Road. Jason was still behind me as I ran across the main road and on into Guilford Street, where I could have ducked left and towards my own house.

Instead, like a complete moron, I went the other way and found myself being closed on by a really angry-looking Jason. He was calling me all kinds of names and people were stopping to watch what was going on, not a single one of them doing anything to help me. Then I saw a little kid, about three, right in my path. He was only a few metres away and I couldn't stop. I would have knocked him down. Instead, I picked him up and then came to a stop. Behind us his mother shouted after me from the front door of their house. I turned and ran back with the kid, who was grinning at me, and handed him over. I mumbled sorry and then I heard Jason hit a wheelie-bin. I turned and ran on, beginning to laugh to myself like a mad man, even though I was bricking it.

I sprinted down another road with big tall Victorian houses on both sides and on past the entrance to a synagogue. I had to stop and catch my breath a bit then, and when I turned I could see Jason, still coming after me and holding some kind of stick in his hands. I set off again, down College Street which is really narrow and has these alleyways on both sides. I ran past a blonde girl walking a fat Rottweiller, not stopping even though she had smiled at me, and then I turned into Prebend Street where I nearly knocked over a policeman.

'Hold on, mate!' said the copper, grabbing me by the jacket.

'Lemme go!'

'Calm down . . . What are you running away from?' he said, all suspicious.

I pushed his hands away and caught my breath.

'Someone's after me,' I said. 'With a stick.' I pointed round the corner and the policeman went to have a look.

'No one here, mate,' he told me.

'But he was *right* behind me,' I said, walking back round the corner.

The street was empty except for the blonde girl who was trying to drag her dog behind her, and she was up near the top of the road.

'No one at all,' said the policeman.

'Must have seen you and done a runner,' I said.

'Would you like to make a report?' he asked but I shook my head.

'Right, well try and be more careful next time – you could have hurt me,' he said.

I looked at him like he was mad.

'Ain't that your job?' I asked. 'Anything to protect the tax-paying public?'

He gave me a really dirty look in return.

'Gotta be off,' I said. 'Me mum's made bacon sandwiches for tea.' And I ran off before he had the chance to grab my jacket again.

* * *

By the time I got in I was soaked and I'd decided that enough was enough. It was time to tell my brother that I needed his help. I walked into the living room expecting to see Gussie lying around on his fat bum as usual. He wasn't in though. My sister was sitting where he normally sat, watching the telly and talking to a friend on the phone at the same time.

'Ooh *yeah*,' she said, into the handset.

'You see Gussie?' I asked.

She gave me a dirty look, covered the mouthpiece with her hand and told me that she was trying to have a conversation.

'Just tell me where Gussie is,' I replied.

'He's out . . . what am I – his *mum*?' she said before turning up the telly *and* chatting into her phone. Girls . . .

SIXTEEN

The next day I found Jit talking to Robert and Wesley at lunch. They were in the computer room with Hannah, Grace, Imi and Suky, and the fantasy twins were *still* talking about that book.

'Princess Wondlebarn used the Shield of Ages to deflect the magic powers of Gerafaggan,' Robert was saying when I joined them.

'And she released Tar from the Dark Way too,' added Wesley.

'So the people of Nebilet are free from the evils of Gerafaggan,' continued Robert.

'What – *for ever*?' I asked, with a smile.

'Well – Gerafaggan *has* escaped into the Void with the Flute of Kings so I assume that there will be a sequel,' replied Robert.

'Oh I should hope so,' said Wesley.

'What *void*?' asked Jit.

'The Void is the no-man's-land between the evil forces and those of the Lighted Path,' Robert explained.

Jit just looked more confused than ever.

'Hang on – you never told me nothing about no Lighted Path!' he said.

'It's there at the very beginning of the book when Time speaks to Princess Wondlebarn and warns her of the evil machinations of her wicked uncle, Gerafaggan, and his dastardly wife, Noreanna,' explained Wesley.

'Sounds like you're making it all up to me,' I said.

Wesley pulled the book from his bag. It was about three times the thickness of a normal book and had a painting on the cover of warlocks and winged horses and a blonde princess with flowing locks.

'There you go,' he said. 'You may borrow it if you like – I'm already reading another.'

'What's the new one about?' I asked, instantly wishing that I hadn't.

'It's the prequel to this one – *Gerafaggan the Glorious*,' said Wesley.

'Man – this is just mad. How many *are* there?' I asked.

'Seven so far,' said Robert. 'The author is writing the eighth as we speak.'

'What, *right* now?' asked Jit.

'I shouldn't be surprised,' replied Robert.

'Nah – them authors got an easy life, you get me? I bet the author's sitting on his backside looking out the window and drinking coffee and that,' said Jit.

I yawned real loud to show him that I was bored of the conversation and headed over to where Hannah was seated at a computer, her fingers tapping away at the keyboard.

'Yo, Sister Aitch, what you doin'?' I asked.

'Working,' she said, not even looking up.

Jit came over and asked me if I'd told Gussie about Jason yet. I told him about Jason chasing after me and about how I hadn't seen Gussie yet.

'I'm going to though,' I said. 'I've had enough of that freak chasing me around with his piggy eyes and butt for a face.'

'Cool – it's about time Gussie taught him some manners anyways,' replied Jit.

'Too right,' I said.

'Man's an idiot . . .' added Jit, as Robert coughed. I ignored him.

'Looks like a monkey anyway,' I said. 'With his hair and mash-up mout' and that.'

I heard the cough again and then Hannah and Grace took a deep breath, at the same time, like they were joined at the hip or something. I turned to see what Robert wanted and came face to face for the second time in twenty-four hours with Jason Patel.

'*Er . . .*' I began.

'I wanna talk to you,' he said. 'Outside, in the corridor.'

I waited for the punch but it never came. I followed Jason out of the room, telling Jit that I'd be all right on my own. It was time to face up to him anyway, I thought to myself. I had to stand up to him, beating or not. I was sick of his bullying.

He turned to me in the corridor and tried to smile. Then I saw the bruises on his face for the first time. Out of the corner of my eye I could see the others pressed up against the glass, all looking worried.

'I got to say summat,' he said, quietly.

'What?' I asked. 'Ain't even like you *paid* for that phone so I don't see how you can ask for no money back.'

'I . . . you . . . the phone is yours.'

'You *what*?'

'You can have the phone, bro. I just wanted to say that . . . well . . . that I'm kinda s-s-sorry and that.'

I looked at him for a minute, expecting to see an ugly grin break on his face and for a left hook to come flying in, but he just stood where he was, looking at the floor. It was then that I realized that he was actually apologizing to me for real. Jason Patel, bully boy number one, saying sorry like he was six and had been caught stealing sweets by his mum. Man, I wanted to laugh.

'If I've ever upset you . . . you know, bullied you and that . . . I was wrong, bro, and well . . .' he continued.

'*What?*' I asked, much more confident now.

'If you ever need anyt'ing or anyone has a go at you . . . just come to me and I'll—'

'You joking?' I asked. I couldn't believe what I was hearing. The man was chasing me round the streets only a few hours earlier and now he was all sheepish and that.

Maybe I'm a bit stupid or maybe I just didn't realize that it was a possibility but I finally worked it out and grinned to myself.

'Anyway, I gave the phone to your brother last night,' he said.

'So you *met* Gussie then . . .?' I asked, smirking.

'Er . . . *yeah*. Anyway I gotta go, bro . . . laters.'

And with that he walked away. I stood where I was for a while, just letting it all sink in. How had Gussie known where to find him anyway and what had he said? My mind was in overdrive. I headed back into the class, smiling.

'What was all *that* about?' asked Grace.

'*Yeah* – what did he want?' added Jit.

'Oh, nuttin' – just wanted to *apologize* to me,' I replied.

'Get *lost*!' said Jit. 'What did he *really* want?'

I shrugged.

'Dunno – just some nonsense about them phones . . . nuttin' serious.'

'But he said he was going to beat you up,' said Hannah.

'Maybe he had a change of heart . . . like, you know, maybe he ran out of guss,' I said with a grin.

'You mean *gas*,' corrected Grace.

'Hey, posh chick – I know what I mean.'

Jit looked at me, grinned, shook his head and then he turned back to Robert and Wesley.

'I got this idea, man . . . *Ganglefart the Goblin and the Witches of Devana* . . . Hannah and Grace is the witches . . .'

When I got home that night, Gussie was in the kitchen with Gramps, reading a newspaper.

'Anything you want to tell me, bro?' I asked, as I sat down.

He grinned.

'*Nah*,' he said, shaking his head. 'Nuttin' really springs to mind . . .'

'You *sure* now?'

'Yeah . . . Oh no, hang on a minute. There *was* this skinny kid I seen last night, running away from some school bully like he was running for his life.'

'You *seen* me?' I asked, amazed.

'So I thought I'd maybe pull the bully up, y'know. Teach him a likkle lesson and that . . . he was only *too* keen to listen to me. And he gave me a likkle something to give to the poor kid he was chasing.' He pulled the phone from his pocket and set it down in front of me.

Now it was my turn to grin and I did, so wide that my Gramps raised an eyebrow at me.

'Yuh ago crack yuh face, bwoi, grinnin' like yuh a win de sweepstake dung a Caymanas.'

'Where?' I asked.

'It's a race track in Kingston,' Gussie told me.

'Oh right . . .'

'Anything you gotta say to me, bro?' he asked.

'Yeah,' I said. 'Next time make sure you get proper gear to sell.'

'Yuh cheeky raas . . .' he replied.

'One time, back in sixty-three,' said Gramps, 'me tek dat bwoi Bob Marley dung de track. Dat bwoi a gamble alla him money pon one stupid 'orse name GullyRat and den 'im waan my money too!' He chuckled to himself at the memory, real or not.

'You what?' I asked, wondering what the hell Gramps was on about.

'Is a nice phone yuh have deh bwoi, you wan' sell it?' he said, forgetting what he had just been talking about, as usual.

For a *moment* I considered it. *Just* for a moment but then I shook my head.

'Nah, Gramps. It don't work anyway.'

Gramps shrugged, farted and then shook his head. I wasn't about to sell the dodgy phone to him or anyone else. I'd learned my lesson. From now on I was going to check anything I sold, myself. I mean, I didn't want to end up on one of them consumer programmes like the *Watchdog* or nothing. I got up and went to use the land line, calling Jit.

'Wanna come over for dinner?' I asked.

'Yeah, man,' he replied.

'You may as well bring your stuff too. You know we're gonna be messing with that Xbox 'til whenever.'

'Cool,' said Jit.

I put the phone down and turned to my gramps.

'You still got all them old tunes in your room, Gramps?' I asked him.

'Yeah, man – why?' he replied, smiling.

'Wanna play me some of them . . . *y'know*, educate de yout' dem.'

'Well, all right,' said Gramps. 'But any more of yuh cheek and yuh ago get—'

'Yeah I know, Gramps . . . *lick dung*!'

I ran before his well aimed cuff could catch my ears.

Two more tales from Devana High

SECRETS

JIT can't be bothered with school. His mum's new boyfriend is doing his head in, and the last thing on his mind is dealing with lessons and homework. He needs the gang's help, and fast . . .

SUKY and Imi have been going out for ages. But there's trouble in paradise – namely, Suky's strict parents. A whole load of drama is about to kick off . . .